Granny nothing

The door was pounded again, and suddenly a voice boomed through it, a deep voice, a bellowing voice. Was it a man? Was it a woman? It was impossible to tell. I only knew it was the most terrifying voice I had ever heard.

"Be careful, Steph!" Ewen whispered.

It was hard to make out anything with the rain lashing against the glass. I could see nothing at first as I peered cautiously closer into the stormy darkness.

Suddenly, a flash of lightning illuminated the sky and there, zooming right in front of me, so close I could make out the hairs in the nose, was the scariest face I had ever seen.

Look out for the next book in this series. . .

Granny Nothing and the Shrunken Head

Granny nothing

Catherine MacPhail
Illustrated by **Sarah Nayler**

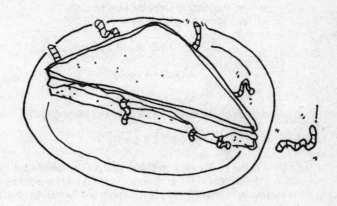

■SCHOLASTIC

For Robert David Cherry,
my first grandchild

Scholastic Children's Books,
Commonwealth House,
1-19 New Oxford Street,
London, WC1A 1NU, UK
a division of Scholastic Ltd
London ~ New York ~ Toronto ~ Sydney ~ Auckland
Mexico City ~ New Delhi ~ Hong Kong

First published by Scholastic Ltd, 2003

ISBN 0 439 98287 1

Typeset by M Rules
Printed and bound by Cox and Wyman Ltd, Reading, Berks

10 9 8 7 6 5 4 3 2 1

Chapter One

The day Granny Nothing came into our lives started off as a perfectly ordinary day.

Well, actually, there was nothing perfect about it. Mum was rushing around as usual, anxious to get off to an important meeting. Dad was stuffing papers into his briefcase. He had an important meeting too. And Nanny Sue, her head wrapped in a towel, was stuffing gooey mush into the baby's mouth, all smiles.

She was all smiles, that is, not the baby. Little Thomas looked as though he was ready to throw up, and he

1

probably would. Hopefully, all over the smiling face of Nanny Sue. I'm Stephanie, by the way, little Thomas's big sister. Not that being his sister is anything to be proud of.

"Now, you're sure you'll be all right?" Mum asked, for the hundredth time.

I wondered what she would say if we answered "No! Don't leave us to the mercy of the horrible Nanny Sue!" Probably she'd say exactly what she did say.

"I promise I'll be home early tomorrow and we'll spend some quality time together."

Quality time – I wonder what that means exactly? I sighed. I'd heard it all before.

"We'll be fine, Mum," I assured her.

"I'll take care of the family." This came from Ewen, my younger brother. Younger in age by a year, in brain power, by at least ten thousand. Walking upright is still a problem for him. He'd been watching his Bruce Willis videos again. "I'll take care of the womenfolk," kind of thing. Take care of the family? He almost faints every time we have to run past next door's Rottweilers.

Baby Thomas gurgled. He still couldn't say a word. I'm convinced that's because his mouth is always full of gooey mush, pushed there by the sadistic Nanny Sue. Mum hugged him close and the goo trickled down her good business suit. That wouldn't worry Mum. She'd go into her meeting like that quite happily. Maybe she wouldn't feel so guilty about leaving us then.

"I'll take good care of them, Mrs McAllister," Nanny Sue said.

Mum hugged her too. She is a terrible one for hugging. And she just loves Nanny Sue. Not a good judge of character, in spite of being the best mum in the world.

"I always feel I'm leaving them with their big sister."

Ewen glanced at me and raised his eyes to heaven. If only Mum knew the truth. Thomas chose that moment to vomit all over Nanny Sue. He might not be able to talk, but he certainly knew how to say the right thing at the right time.

What a baby!

Nanny Sue, her face covered in vomit, kept right on smiling. It was amazing how she could do that even when she was seething inside.

"Well, wish me luck this morning," Dad said, standing with his briefcase tucked under his arm. He looked like a schoolboy going off for an exam. But we all knew it was more important than that. He'd been up half the night working on a new project for his boss, Mr Dangerfield. He'd only just started in this job and he was very keen to impress him. "If he likes this, it could mean a promotion, more money." He smiled. "We'll book a holiday." That made us all smile. Then he beamed at Nanny Sue. "You can come too," he told her. Our smiles disappeared, and the baby began to wail.

"Come on, Paula." Dad pulled Mum on. "Can't afford to be late today."

"Must fly!" Mum said and gave us all another round of hugs, collecting more goo in the process. And then they were both gone.

As soon as he saw her go, Thomas began to wail even louder. He knew what he was in for.

Nanny Sue's smile disappeared. "Shut up, you!" she snapped at Thomas, dislodging vomit from her eye and slapping it on Thomas's head. "I'm going to make you very sorry you did that."

"Don't talk to my little brother like that," Ewen yelled at her.

Nanny Sue sniggered. "And what are you going to do about it, big man? Get your friend Todd Dangerfield on to me? I know he does everything you ask."

Ewen's shoulders slumped. He wouldn't say anything else now. Nanny Sue knew that Todd Dangerfield made Ewen's life a misery at school. He picked on him mercilessly. Ewen never did anything about it, and Nanny Sue knew why. Todd Dangerfield's father was our dad's new boss. Dad had been out of work for so long, and was so happy to get this job, so determined to make good in it for all our sakes. Todd Dangerfield knew he could do anything to Ewen and he would just let him. Nanny Sue knew it, too, and relished it. She was nasty, was Nanny Sue. She WAS like a big sister. One of the ugly sisters in Cinderella, in fact both of them. A horrible big sister you can't get rid of. However, we usually managed to get our own back on her. Like today.

Suddenly, she whipped the towel from her head with an angry flourish.

"OK. Which one of you did this!"

Ewen and I immediately fell about laughing. Her hair, usually pale gold, was bright red. Bright, brick red. In fact it looked as if it was on fire. It was standing out in petrified tufts all over her head. Nanny Sue didn't see the joke.

"Which one of you swapped my shampoo for this awful hair dye?" She began stamping her feet like a baby. "Who did it!!!!" she yelled.

"It was Ewen's idea," I told her. "But don't give him all the credit. I chose the colour, so I suppose you can thank both of us."

We looked at each other and giggled. Nanny Sue was furious. She shook her flaming red hair in anger and Baby Thomas was walloped with a mouthful.

"I'm going to tell your mum and dad!" Nanny Sue screamed.

"Tell them then." I threw it right back at her. "And we'll tell them how lazy you are. You're always doing your make-up and fixing your hair, and painting your nails. Not that it does any good. You're still as ugly as sin."

"I'm too beautiful to be a nanny," she yelled, waving her hair about. "One day, I am going to be rich and famous! I should be a star."

Nanny Sue had dreams of being a celebrity. "Well, now you've got hair that will get you noticed," I told her.

"You two are horrible to me," she screeched.

"You're horrible to us," Ewen reminded her.

"You were horrible first."

"No we were not."

"Yes you were so!"

And so it went on back and forth till Nanny Sue finally shouted at the top of her voice. "You two, get ready for school!" We jumped at once. "And as for you. . ." She turned her attention to Thomas. He spat out her hair and gurgled, trying to look sweet and innocent. It would never work with Nanny Sue. Even at nine months he should have learned that. She lifted him from his chair. "You're going to have a bath," she said.

Baby Thomas screeched. His eyes crossed in horror. Baths were his worst nightmare. He hated them. I'm sure he must have been a cat in his past life, because no baby could hate water that much.

"We should tell Mum and Dad about her," Ewen said as we left the house.

"She would only blame us." We'd done so many nasty things to Nanny Sue since she came, no wonder she hated us. But she was lazy and bad-tempered and stupid and it brightened up our lives no end thinking of what tricks we could play on her next.

"Remember the time we put itching powder in her knickers?" Ewen remembered fondly.

"And then there was that time we swapped her moisturizer for hair-removing cream."

"Her eyebrows disappeared . . . and so did her eyelashes. She looked like an alien." Ewen had loved that one, especially because Nanny Sue was going out on a big date that night. The guy had taken one look at her, made an excuse to make a phone call, and she hadn't seen him since!

We giggled fondly at the memories.

But no matter what we did, nothing was going to get rid of her. "Who would look after us if she left?" I said to Ewen. "You of all people should know how hard Dad is trying in this new job. It took him so long to get it, and he can't risk losing it. And Mum can't lose hers until she's sure Dad's going to be kept on. They need someone to look after us. And if we have to put up with Nanny Sue so they don't have to worry about something else, then we will!"

I said it defiantly.

Ewen tutted. "I don't suppose things are that bad," he said, banging the front door behind him. That's when he realized how wrong he was. Things couldn't be much worse. The banging of the door was all the warning next door's Rottweilers, Hannibal and Lecter, needed.

They popped their heads above the fence. Their eyes lit up, they started to growl. They were looking forward to this just as they did every morning. Ewen and I were their exercise routine for the day.

Never one to waste an opportunity, Nanny Sue used the diversion to put the rubbish out in the bin. "Hope they catch you this time!" she shouted, before dashing back inside the safety of the house.

"Run for it!" Ewen screamed, and already his breath was coming in short bursts. He'd need his inhaler before we made that bus . . . if we made that bus. I was already away, racing down the path ahead of him, and he was just centimetres ahead of the galloping dogs. I saw the bus coming, right on time. I glanced at next door's gate. It was tight shut. Relief. They had never yet made it over, but one day I knew that those dogs would learn to jump that gate. One day the bus wouldn't be quite on time. One day . . . we were going to be the dogs' dinner.

But not today.

This, then, was a perfectly ordinary day in the life of the McAllister family.

Ordinary, that is, until eight o'clock that night, when it was dark and stormy.

And Granny Nothing arrived.

Chapter Two

The storm was raging outside. Rain lashed against the windows, the wind howled through the telegraph wires, and every few minutes there was an ear-shattering crack of thunder. I was scared. I'm terrified of thunder, but what frightened me more was the fact that Mum and Dad hadn't come home yet. They always tried to arrive home before we were marched off to bed by Nanny Sue so she could watch one of her soppy programmes on TV. What could be keeping them tonight?

"Do you think they'll be OK?" I asked Nanny Sue.

"Didn't I tell you?" she answered, with a wicked grin. She still hadn't forgiven us for the red hair. It looked even brighter in the firelight. "They're not coming back. They've had enough of you. So, that means . . . I'll be taking care of you all for the rest of your lives."

Suddenly, it wasn't just the thunder that was terrifying me.

"That's not true!" Ewen yelled. "Mum and Dad would never do that."

His voice trembled a little, though, as if he wasn't quite sure.

"Wouldn't they?" Nanny Sue giggled. Horrible sound it was. "If they liked you that much, do you think they'd work such long hours, and leave you here with me?"

She knew the right things to say, did Nanny Sue.

"I want to stay up till they come in." I decided I was going to insist on that.

Nanny Sue almost flew at me. "Over my dead body. You're all going to bed right now. *Star-Maker* is on telly, and I intend to watch it alone."

Star-Maker was a programme where pop hopefuls auditioned live in front of a panel of so-called experts who then tore their efforts to ribbons. Most of the contestants were really rubbish and it was a great laugh watching them making such fools of themselves. But every so often a star really did emerge. It was brilliant television and Nanny Sue loved it. She saw herself as one of the stars!

Baby Thomas gurgled. He'd be quite happy to be

packed off to bed just to get away from her. He should have kept quiet. His gurgling reminded her he was there.

"And as for you, you little horror, you'll finish the very last bit of your supper before you go."

Unfortunately, the last bits of Tom's supper were lodged in the crevices of his pelican bib. His eyes crossed again and a look of utter horror passed across the baby's face as she scooped and scraped the contents on to a spoon.

"Ugh! You can't give him that!"

Nanny Sue glared at Ewen. "Do you want it instead?" She pressed her face right up to Ewen's. Ewen shrank back.

"Thought not," she said, and with that she stuffed the revolting mess right into poor Baby Tom's mouth.

I began to yell at her. "I hate you! I wish someone would come along so we could get rid of you. Anyone! No matter how horrible they were they would have to be better than you! I WISH! I WISH! I WISH!"

At that very moment there was a loud banging on the front door. I yelped. Ewen froze to the floor. Baby Tom took the opportunity to spew the contents of his mouth all over Nanny Sue. As she was vegetarian and the goo was chicken, she wasn't best pleased.

"You little horror!" she screamed, and she looked round at my brother and me. "You're all little horrors. Do you know who that is?"

The door was pounded again. The house seemed to shudder. Nanny Sue grinned. A grin that would have done justice to a skeleton. "That's the bogeyman. And he's come to get you for being nasty to me."

As if in answer the banging began again, even louder and more persistent. It sounded as if the door was ready to collapse, as if a stampeding elephant was trying to force its way in.

"It's probably Mum," I said to Ewen, trying to reassure him, and myself. "She's forgotten her key."

"You don't really believe that," Nanny Sue said, heading for the door. "Now you'll be sorry."

The door was pounded again, and suddenly a voice boomed through it, a deep voice, a bellowing voice. Was it a man? Was it a woman? It was impossible to tell. I only knew it was the most terrifying voice I had ever heard.

"Hell's Bells and Buckets! Is somebody going to let me in!"

Now it was Nanny Sue who froze to the spot. The door was pounded again. There was a crack of thunder. I decided to show old Nanny Sue I had more gumption than she did. I tiptoed closer. There was a little window on the door with a small net curtain over it. Warily, I swallowed and moved the curtain back a centimetre.

"Be careful, Steph!" Ewen whispered.

It was hard to make out anything with the rain lashing against the glass. I could see nothing at first as I peered cautiously closer into the stormy darkness.

Suddenly, a flash of lightning illuminated the sky and there, zooming right in front of me, so close I could make out the hairs in the nose, was the scariest face I had ever seen.

I screamed. Ewen screamed. Nanny Sue screamed.

A roar came from the other side of the door. "Will you open this door! I'm getting drown-ded out here!"

I began to shake. Ewen moved beside me and I could feel him shaking too.

"Are. . . Are. . . Are. . ." Ewen could hardly get the words out. But I knew what he wanted to ask.

"Are you the bogeyman?" I wailed.

There was a loud guffaw. It was hard to tell if it was a laugh or a roar.

"God love ye, of course I'm not the bogeyman. Don't be so daft."

I forced myself to sound bold. "Well, who are you then?"

Another explosion of thunder rent the air before the answer came. An answer that sent shivers of fear through me.

"I'm your granny."

Nanny Sue gave me a push. "That's your granny?" she asked in disbelief.

"No. She is not," I shouted. Anger was taking the place of fear now. How dare this monstrous creature claim to be our granny! I pressed my face boldly against the glass. "No. You are not. Our granny's in Arizona."

The horrible face came so close to mine that I started to shake again.

"I'm your other granny. Your daddy's mammy."

I turned to Ewen. I was horrified. "Did she say . . . our daddy's . . . mammy?"

Dad hardly ever talked about his mother. And whenever we asked about her, both he and Mum always exchanged secret glances and changed the subject. She had emigrated, we were told. He'd lost contact with her, he would tell us. But once Ewen and I had heard him whispering to Mum when he thought we'd gone to bed. "No wonder I lost contact with her. She's a monster." Now it seemed the monster was right here in front of us, peering through the glass. Could this horrible creature possibly be our dad's mother? If she was, no wonder he called her a monster. She wasn't human. My dad must have been raised by a gang of wild gorillas somewhere. And since the creature spoke with a strong Scottish accent, the wild gorillas must have been based near Glasgow. I'd heard it was a jungle up there anyway.

"Are you going to let me in!" the creature yelled again. "This is a terrible way to treat family."

Ewen jumped up then. "How do we know you're telling the truth? You could be anybody."

For a moment there was no reply, then suddenly, a photograph was pressed against the pane. "There! Is that proof enough?"

We peered at the damp photograph. It was an old colour snapshot of two people and one of them was most certainly Dad. A schoolboy Dad, in his uniform, looking glum and mortified. Beside him, as proud as punch, was the horrible creature, dressed in a pink fluffy suit and a pink hat. I had never seen anything that so closely resembled a rhinoceros in my life. A rhinoceros wrapped in candyfloss.

This was our granny!

"Let me in!" Her screech came at the same time as another crack of thunder. She was louder than thunder could ever be.

"We are not letting her in." Nanny Sue's voice quivered. She held the baby in front of her for protection. "She could be an axe murderer. And they always go for the young and beautiful ones first . . . and that means ME!"

I looked at Ewen. That decided us. We opened the door, and let her in.

Chapter Three

In the doorway stood the most enormous woman I had ever seen. A woman? Well, she was wearing a dress, but there the resemblance to anything female ended. Her hair was stuffed into a Rainmate, with tufts sticking out all over the place. Her coat was too tight and bits of her were oozing out through the buttonholes as if her body was trying to escape. She was dripping all over the floor. She looked more like a wet unmade bed than anything else.

"What a blinkin' night," she wheezed, and she shook herself like a dog. Everyone took a step back to stop getting soaked but not far enough to be missed when she let out a stomach-churning sneeze a moment later and covered us all with something more disgusting than rain.

"Get me a basin of hot water for my feet. Oh, I'm a martyr to these feet."

What a cheek! A perfect stranger, in the door ten seconds and demanding basins of water. I would have told her "No!" right then, but there was something really scary about this creature. Nanny Sue felt it too. She was off and into the kitchen for the hot water before you could say "axe murderer".

"Who's she?" the creature demanded.

"She's our nanny," Ewen said softly. The baby yelled.

"A nanny! That son of mine's got you a nanny?" She looked at Thomas. "Aye, no wonder you're yelling. I don't like her at all."

She laid her battered suitcase on the floor and took off her coat and threw it on the sofa. The suitcase, I noticed, was covered with labels from all sorts of exotic places. Bogota, Hawaii, Nepal, Craigmillar. Then she threw herself on to the sofa too. I was amazed it didn't break in half.

"Are you really our granny?" Ewen dared to ask.

Her face broke into a smile. Oh dear, she didn't have very many teeth and the ones she had were a very odd colour.

"Course I am. Thought it was about time you met me." Even when she was trying to be nice, she roared.

I wanted to ask why we hadn't met her before. But I

decided then that I'd ask Dad. I glanced at my brother, warned him with my eyebrows not to ask her anything either. He knew what I meant. He'd been reading my eyebrows for years.

Nanny Sue returned then with a basin of steaming water. We all watched in amazement as the creature rolled down her stockings from her knees and dropped them on the floor. I thought I was going to be sick. I'd never seen feet like that in my life. The toes were massive and bent over each other, and there were great horny corns growing on them. She sank them into the water and let out a satisfied groan.

"Aw, that's better. You take care of your feet and your feet will take care of you."

I looked again at her feet. She called that taking care of them?

Her gaze settled fondly on my brother. "And you must be Ewen. You look just like your daddy when he was a boy." Ewen took a step back. I didn't blame him. She looked as if she was about to hug him. Then she turned her toothy smile on me.

"And you . . . are you Stephanie? Och, I would have known you anywhere. It's like looking into a mirror. You're the spitting image of myself."

Time stood still. I almost screamed. Inside I did scream. Me? The spitting image of this monster? The creature was mad.

"So, what are we supposed to call you?" Ewen asked her after a moment. "Our other granny is called Granny Fielding. She's our mum's mum. So you must be. . .?"

He thought about it for a moment, and shrugged. "Granny McAllister?"

Her face went almost the same colour as Nanny Sue's hair. "Me? Och no, darlin'. I'm too young to be called Granny."

Too young to be called Granny? That was ridiculous. She was about the oldest woman I had ever seen. If she was a woman that is, I still wasn't sure. She looked more like a rhinoceros in a frock. And there was no way I looked like a rhinoceros in a frock.

In fact, I had to blink to make sure she wasn't a rhinoceros.

"Granny indeed!" she went on gruffly. The image of the rhinoceros shimmered and she became the strange creature on the sofa again. "Granny Nothing, if you don't mind."

Granny Nothing? It was as good a name for her as any, I decided.

And anyway, she wouldn't be here long enough for us to call her anything. Because, as soon as Dad came home he'd send this Granny Nothing back to wherever she'd come from.

And that was how Mum and Dad found her when they did come home, still with her feet in water and with me and Ewen and the baby all staring at her. Nanny Sue was in a corner, shaking like a jellyfish.

I couldn't get over Dad's face when he saw her there. Shock! Horror! Rage! He threw down his briefcase and almost yelled. "How did you find me?"

And Granny Nothing asked the very question that came to my mind. "Were you hiding from me then?"

So, she was our granny after all. With that thought, I started to shake like a jellyfish. This horrible creature, our granny!

Mum, noticing her children were all still up, turned her anger on Nanny Sue. "Why aren't they in bed? Take Thomas up right now! He should have been sleeping hours ago."

Nanny Sue lifted the baby from his chair and he immediately began to wail.

"A nanny!" Granny Nothing almost spat the words out. "What are my grandchildren doing with a nanny?"

"I don't know what I'd do without her!" Mum said, and she flashed a forgiving smile at Nanny Sue. Thomas wailed even louder. Nanny Sue was probably nipping him under his blanket. "She's a wonder," Mum said, daring Granny Nothing to disagree with her.

Granny Nothing did. "A wonder? I wonder what she's doing here. She's a wimp. She should never have let me in. I could have been anybody. I could have been an axe murderer."

And she probably had been at some point, I thought.

"She showed me a photograph," Nanny Sue said, defending herself. "It was you and her, Mr McAllister."

Granny Nothing's voice became suddenly sentimental. "It was your confirmation, son. Do you remember?"

Dad snapped back at her. "How could I forget. You assaulted the bishop."

"He slapped your face. Nobody touches my boy."

"He was supposed to," Dad reminded her. "That's what happens at confirmation."

"Well, you're not going to need a nanny now. I'm here. I'll look after them."

Ewen and I gasped. I had thought anyone would be better than Nanny Sue. Now, Nanny Sue seemed warm and loving and safe. I managed a smile in her direction. She even managed to smile back.

"You can't let her take over from me," Nanny Sue wailed. She hugged Thomas close. He wailed too. "I love these children . . . and they love me."

That was more than an exaggeration. It was a downright lie. But at that moment I wasn't going to disagree. "See, even Thomas is crying at the thought of losing me."

Dad snapped. "Don't worry about a thing, Sue. You are not in any danger of losing your job. She's not staying." Dad looked at Mum. "Get the children to bed, Paula. I want to talk to her."

Then he turned his attention back to Granny Nothing and his voice changed. "As for you, I want to know what you think you're doing here!"

She flashed him an almost toothless smile. "I wanted to meet my grandchildren. They're lovely, son. I thought I might spend some time getting to know them."

Dad's face went a strange shade of green. It took him a moment to answer. "You can stay here tonight. But that's all. You can sleep in Nanny Sue's room."

At that point there was a strangled cry from Nanny Sue. "In . . . with me?"

Dad ignored her. He was too busy with Granny Nothing. "But after that you'll have to find somewhere else to stay. Understand?"

It was a terrible way to speak to your mother. But then, this Granny Nothing didn't look as if she could possibly be anybody's mother.

Reluctantly, I climbed the stairs to my bedroom. How I wished I could stay and listen to that conversation, but I lingered at the top of the stairs long enough to hear Granny Nothing say, "Are you still ashamed of me, son?"

"Is she really our granny?" I asked Mum when she came in to say goodnight.

Mum sighed. "I'm afraid she is."

"Then why have we never met her?"

Mum had to think about that. Making up an answer. A lie. "She lives very far away. She moves around all the time," she said at last.

"She knew all about us. Who I was, who Ewen was."

"Of course she does. There has been some contact with her. Postcards now and then. . ."

Funny they hadn't told us about them.

"And is Dad ashamed of her?"

It took her even longer to think of an answer to that one. Finally, she lied, "Of course he isn't. It's simply that they never really got on."

Ewen crept into my bedroom when Mum had gone. "I'd be ashamed of her if she was my mother."

We could hear the voices drifting up from downstairs. Angry voices, although we couldn't make out what was being said. There was a mystery here. Dad was a really nice man, everyone liked him, and he liked everybody. So why didn't he like his own mother? I shrugged the thought away.

"I'm not going to worry about it," I said, pulling the covers up to my chin. "We'll never have to see her again. She'll be gone in the morning."

But, she wasn't.

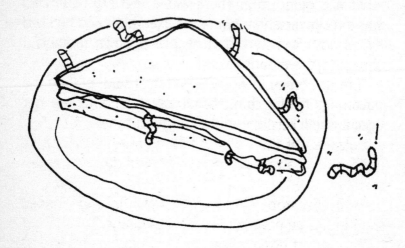

Chapter Four

By the time we came down for breakfast Dad and Mum had already left. Left in anger. We had listened upstairs as Dad told Granny Nothing that she could stay at the house for the day, but when he came home from work they would speak about this. "It's impossible for you to stay. You must see that!"

She obviously didn't. "Why not?"

Dad stammered. "Because . . . because. . ." He was struggling for a reason. "We don't have any room for you."

"Get rid of that wimp of a nanny and I'll sleep in her room."

"I could never do without Nanny Sue!" Mum jumped into the conversation with a vengeance.

"Your children could," came Granny Nothing's reply. "They don't like her."

"They do. They love her."

Granny Nothing let out a bellow of laughter. "Hell's Bells and Buckets! Can you not see that they don't?"

I glanced at Ewen. Wasn't it strange that she had noticed right away what our mum and dad had never seen?

"Will you stop that swearing!" Mum was almost shouting. "I've never heard such language."

"You've just not met the right people."

And so it went on, arguing back and forth until Mum and Dad banged out of the front door and roared off in the car.

Granny Nothing was sitting at the table reading the paper when we went into the kitchen. Nanny Sue came in behind us, still carrying a wailing Thomas.

"You'd better go today!" she moaned. "You certainly can't sleep in my room again. I've never heard such snoring." With that she plucked out her earplugs. "I had to wear these all night. And I still didn't get any sleep."

So that's what the sound was? Granny Nothing's snoring. I'd thought it was rumbling thunder.

"Didn't wake me up," Granny Nothing said. "Anyway, it wasn't half as bad as your singing."

Nanny Sue began to choke. She was convinced she was a wonderful singer. Ewen and I had always told her she was. Always trying to get her to write in to *Star-Maker*, so we could both have a good laugh at her. "I'll have you know one day my voice will bring me fame and fortune," she said airily.

Granny Nothing didn't even look up from her paper. "Aye, you'll be the first person put in the jail for murdering a song." Then she opened her mouth and laughed heartily.

Nanny Sue ignored that. "I need my full eight hours." She was almost in tears. "Or I'm just so bad-tempered all day."

"You're bad-tempered anyway," I reminded her.

Thomas wailed even louder.

"Shut up, you!" she yelled at him.

Granny Nothing put her paper down. "Why is that wee baby always crying?"

"Because he's a spoiled little brat," Nanny Sue dared to say, sticking him into his high chair.

"No he is not!" I said. I wanted to add, "He doesn't like you, Nanny Sue, that's why he's always crying" – but that would have sounded as if I was on Granny Nothing's side, and I wasn't. I didn't like her either.

"What's that you're eating?" Granny Nothing asked, watching in disgust as I poured cereal into a bowl.

"It's muesli," I tutted. Didn't she know anything?

"Mooslie? Yuch. I've seen tastier-looking stuff at the bottom of a budgie's cage."

Thomas giggled as if he understood, but his giggle became a wail as a sickly green goo was shoved into his mouth.

"And what on earth are you giving him?" Granny Nothing asked.

Nanny Sue replied primly, "Prune, honey and spinach breakfast. It's very healthy."

Granny Nothing peered into the baby's face. "You don't like it, son. Do you?"

I held my breath waiting for Thomas to wail even louder. I expected it. We all did. I would certainly wail if that ugly face had come so close to mine at breakfast. Granny Nothing might have looked pretty scary last night, but in the cold morning light she was uglier than ever. She seemed to have grown warts and moles overnight. They were all over the place.

Yet instead, Baby Thomas smiled. Then his smile became a giggle, and then his giggle became a loud bellow of laughter. His chubby little fists beat at the table on his chair.

Granny Nothing bellowed back. "Aye, you don't like it!"

"And what do you eat for breakfast?" Nanny Sue asked. "Iron bars?"

Maybe that's how she lost her teeth, I thought.

Granny Nothing smiled. She seemed to have several more of them missing this morning, I noticed. Boy, she was one ugly woman.

There was no way I looked like her!

"What do I like for breakfast? Now, let me think." She

27

didn't have to think for long. "Worms!" she shouted, as if she was going to impress us all. Only she pronounced it "wurums"!

"Wurums? I mean . . . worms?" I said in disbelief.

"Worms?" Ewen looked sick.

Baby Thomas giggled.

"That's disgusting!" said Nanny Sue.

"I've eaten many strange things in my travels. Maggots and bugs and all sorts of creepy-crawlies."

In her travels? Where could she possibly have been to eat things like that? I remembered then that suitcase of hers and all those exotic labels.

No! She was kidding us. She had to be.

"Ah, but there's nothing to beat a nice plate of wurums for breakfast. Mind you, you've got to eat them fast or they wriggle right off your plate!"

I stopped eating my muesli. I felt sick.

"Or a wurum sandwich for your supper," Granny Nothing went on. "Or . . ." she licked her lips, "a nice wurum pie for your tea."

Nanny Sue turned green. "Mr and Mrs McAllister won't like you talking like that."

Thomas giggled even louder. Granny Nothing peered close to him again. "You'd like them better than that goo, wouldn't you, my lovely boy?"

Thomas giggled and seemed to nod in answer.

Suddenly, to everyone's surprise Granny Nothing began to sing. At least I think it was meant to be singing. It was more of a deep tuneless roar like a ship's siren with a bad cold.

"I like wurums, I like wurums,
That's what I like to eat.
I like the way they wriggle in your belly,
Make it wobble like a jelly,
When they're juicy and fat and sweet."

And her belly really was wobbling. Was it filled with worms right this minute? Were they all wriggling about inside her? Perhaps she'd raided the garden early this morning.

The picture that brought to mind made me feel sicker than ever.

Granny Nothing was laughing like a hyena now, and so was the baby.

"Will I sing it again, love?" And with that she picked Thomas up from his chair and began wobbling round the room doing the most disgusting belly dance I had ever seen.

"I like wurums, I like wurums,
That's what I like to eat.
I like the way they wriggle in your belly,
Make it wobble like a jelly,
When they're juicy and fat and ever so . . . sweet."

I was never so glad to be going off to school.

Even passing next door's hounds seemed less terrifying than Granny Nothing.

"Do you think she really does. . ." Ewen hesitated. Didn't want to put his fear into words. "Eat worms?"

29

"Of course she doesn't," I said at once. I was a year older and it was my duty to assure my brother there was nothing to be afraid of. But there was a real doubt in my mind.

This woman was capable of anything.

She was scary, Granny Nothing.

Chapter Five

Ewen had a bad day at school. Todd Dangerfield made him do his homework again.

"And no mistakes this time, or I'll give you a black eye!"

"You should tell Mr Bassett about him," I told Ewen as we watched Todd swagger off with his friends. Mr Bassett was the headmaster, bald as a billiard ball, hence his nickname, Baldy Bassett. "He'd get into terrible trouble. Baldy's always saying he won't tolerate bullying in his school."

Ewen sighed, and stuffed Todd's jotter into his rucksack. "No, Steph, what he actually says is, he doesn't have a bullying problem in his school. He sticks his bald head in the sand and pretends it isn't there!"

Yes, that was true.

"Anyway," Ewen went on. "If I tell on Todd, he'll tell his dad, and his dad will fire our dad and. . ." his voice trailed off. It was hopeless. We both knew it. So did Todd Dangerfield.

We trudged home from school not in the best of moods. To make things worse the Hounds of the Baskervilles were free and roaming round next door's garden.

"Don't run," I warned Ewen softly, "that way they know you're afraid of them."

"They already know I'm afraid of them," Ewen reminded me.

The Rottweilers looked up as we tried to tiptoe past the hedge. Their ears picked up. They growled. They bared their teeth as they spotted us. I could almost see a speech bubble emerging from their heads.

"DINNER!" it said.

"We could be in the house in two minutes," I whispered to Ewen.

"Or in their jaws in one and a half."

"They've never caught us yet," I said, and with a wild spurt I was off, pulling Ewen behind me. I wasn't going to let two dumb dogs get the better of me. "Run!" I screamed.

The Rottweilers seemed to think I was talking to them. They ran.

"We'll never make it. They're gaining on us." Ewen glanced behind him. They were so close he could see the drool dribbling from their jaws.

"They'll never be able to jump the fence," I yelled.

At that moment one of them did. Hannibal.

"Oh no!" Ewen began to run even faster. He was terrified, sure Hannibal was going to catch him. He swung his schoolbag hard against the dog and its contents spilled all over the pavement.

It was the schoolbag that saved us. Hannibal stopped chasing us and began burrowing his nose into the bag. Lecter, thinking there must be something juicy in there, stopped too, and began struggling with a jotter already gripped firmly in Hannibal's jaws.

Ewen and I put on a final spurt and made it to our own gate. We were through it in a flash, racing up the garden path and round to the back door.

We were breathless, but jubilant.

"Made it!" I punched the air.

"Stupid dogs!" Ewen was laughing too, then, suddenly his face fell. "Oh no!"

"Oh no, what?"

"Todd Dangerfield's homework jotter. That's what they were eating."

But the thought of what Todd Dangerfield might do to him was forgotten in an instant as we heard a strange wail coming from the garden. It was the weirdest sound I had ever heard and we both knew at once what it was.

Granny Nothing's singing.

"Oh no, she's still here," I wailed.

"And I thought things couldn't get any worse."

I pushed open the door into the back garden. There she was. She had Baby Thomas with her. He was sitting on a blanket and Granny Nothing was standing over him and dancing. And what was worse, Baby Thomas was loving it. I had never heard him giggle so much before. I had never seen him look so happy.

"I like wurums, I like wurums,
That's what I like to eat.
I like the way they wriggle in your belly,
Make it wobble like a jelly –"

And at that she wobbled her belly and the baby rolled right over, he was laughing so much.

"When they're juicy and fat and sweet."

She bent and picked Thomas up and held him high in the air. The baby's mouth was covered in dirt, and he was dribbling on to Granny Nothing's face. Now she was giggling.

I looked at Ewen in horror. Ewen looked at me.

The same thought occurred to both of us at the same time.

Had she been feeding Baby Thomas . . . worms?

It certainly looked like it. And the baby was loving it.

"Hell's Bells!" she was shouting, with a big gumsy grin. "You're a lovely boy. I could just eat you."

I gasped. So did Ewen.

I began to laugh nervously. "Don't be silly, Ewen. She couldn't possibly mean it."

Then Granny Nothing licked her lips and said it again. "I could just eat you."

"Oh yes she could," Ewen whispered.

This granny was capable of anything.

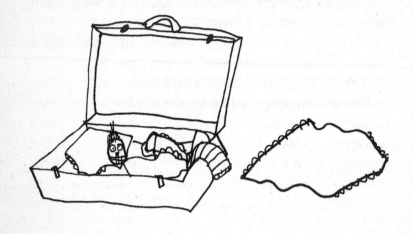

Chapter Six

"She wouldn't actually eat him," Ewen said, with as much conviction as he could muster.

"Of course not," I assured him.

"Wouldn't she?" He didn't sound in the least bit reassured. "She did say she'd eaten a lot of strange things in her travels."

There was nothing else for it. We were going to have to do a little snooping. So while Granny Nothing was in the garden with Thomas we crept into Nanny Sue's room and from underneath the sofa bed we dragged Granny Nothing's old battered suitcase.

Australia. Hackensack. Bogota. Alaska. Echelfechan. Strange-sounding names. She couldn't actually have been to all those places, surely. She'd probably bought the case, with the stickers already attached, at a car boot sale. We snapped the case open. And gasped. It was like Ali Baba's treasure cave. Stuffed inside an alligator handbag there were clogs from Holland. There was a cowboy hat, and a lasso. There was even a grass skirt. On top of them all there lay a photograph of a Spanish bullfighter. It was signed "To my dear amiga, even though you were supposed to fight the bull, not help it escape! I love you anyway. Olé! Jose."

I stared at Ewen my mouth wide open. "She wrote it herself. I bet."

"Look at this." Ewen lifted something that was massive and pink and silk. He held it high. "She must have gone camping, but it's a funny-looking tent."

I snapped it away from him. "It's not a tent, stupid. It's a pair of her knickers. You've just never seen any that size."

Ewen wiped his hands frantically on his shirt and pretended to be sick. "I've touched her knickers. Yuch!"

But I had forgotten her knickers. I had seen what was lying underneath them. "Oh, no! Ewen, look at this."

Ewen gasped with shock. "That's not what I think it is, is it?"

I nodded dumbly. It was exactly what he thought it was, and I was horrified.

Granny Nothing had a Shrunken Head in her case.

We scrabbled frantically to the other side of the room as if the head would suddenly come alive and bite us. We didn't say a word for a minute, just stared at one another in shock.

"A woman who could carry a Shrunken Head about with her is capable of anything," I said at last.

We were both seeing the same picture. Granny Nothing eyeing Thomas hungrily and licking her lips. For all we knew she had lived with a tribe of cannibals and had developed a taste for human flesh! (Well, Thomas was nearly human.) Yes, she could eat him. And probably would. But first, she had filled him up with worms. Her very own worm pie! UGH!

We'd read enough fairy tales about old women who fed children up, got them nice and plump, and then stuffed them into ovens.

It wasn't worth the risk to Thomas, we decided. If Granny Nothing was still here tomorrow, Baby Thomas was not leaving our sight.

And she was. When Dad and Mum had come home they took Granny Nothing into the living room and told her that after talking things through they had decided that she could stay with us, but just for a few days, and then they would help her find somewhere else to live.

"It is his mother," I whispered to Ewen as we listened

sneakily at the top of the stairs. "He can't just throw her out, I suppose."

But deep down we both wished she would go. She was scary.

So once more Granny Nothing tucked herself up on the sofa bed in Nanny Sue's room. And Nanny Sue wasn't happy about it at all.

"I haven't had a wink of sleep . . . again!" she moaned when Ewen and I went downstairs next morning. The house was shuddering with Granny Nothing's snores. So it was easy to put the suggestion to Nanny Sue that we would take the baby away for the day.

Nanny Sue looked very unhappy. If I had liked her even the least little bit I might have felt sorry for her. As it was I just kept imagining what she might look like with a shrunken head. An improvement in my opinion. She was still wearing earplugs and she had great dark circles under her eyes. Either that or her mascara had run.

"I'm never going to catch up on my beauty sleep," she told us, tearfully. As if we cared.

"Well, there you are then," I said with a grin. "You go back to bed and have a good sleep, all day, and we'll look after Thomas." I patted her shoulder as if she really was my beloved big sister. How she couldn't see through me I don't know. But then, Nanny Sue was thick as a brick.

"He's supposed to be coming with me," Nanny Sue said. "All day," she added in disgust. Obviously not looking forward to the prospect.

"Nobody needs to know," I coaxed her.

"And you need the break. You work too hard, Nanny Sue." Ewen was a good actor, I decided. He sounded so convincing.

He certainly convinced Nanny Sue, but of course, as I've said, she was an idiot.

"Yes, I do, don't I? I'm supposed to pick up the camcorder I ordered today. And I had hoped to go to the hairdresser to do something about this hair. . ." she said, dreamily, thinking of a day's "shop till you drop" in town. "But aren't you two meant to be at school?"

"It's an in-service day for teachers." I must be a good actor too. Ewen believed me.

"Is it really?" he asked. I glared at him.

"But remember," Nanny Sue warned us. "I didn't want to give him up. You insisted. Right?"

"Cross my heart," I assured her, making sure, of course that my fingers were crossed at the same time.

We sneaked Thomas out before Granny Nothing was awake. We could hear her snoring as we tiptoed downstairs. We could still hear her snoring as we crept down the path, safely past Hannibal and Lecter for once. In fact, Ewen was sure he could still hear her snoring as we waited for the bus into town.

"You're imagining things," I told him. "It's traffic you hear." Still, as I listened to the steady droning sound coming from somewhere close, I thought he just might be right.

It began to rain while we were on the bus and by the time we reached the park it was pouring down. All morning it rained and rained, and all we could do was sit in a grotty shed and watch the ground get soggier and soggier.

Baby Thomas was having a wonderful time. We had, unfortunately, sat him in his pram under a drip which he was catching on his nose and licking off. The water from the rusty roof was dark brown. It was absolutely filthy! This seemed to make a difference to Thomas. It was, obviously, just clean water he hated.

We didn't notice what he was doing until poor happy Thomas was dark brown too.

"Oh dear, look at the state of him," I cried.

Things got even worse when the sun came out and the rain stopped. We took Thomas out of his pram to sit on a swing and he fell off and splashed right into a puddle. Before we could get to him, he was off. Thomas was the fastest crawler in the baby world. Off he went as we hurried after him, through puddles and soaking grass, getting wetter and wetter and dirtier and dirtier.

"Look at the state of him now!" I wailed, catching up with him at last and lifting him.

"And look at you," Ewen told me. Now I was every bit as bad, with mud and dirt and grass all over me.

A rather stern lady passed and snorted, "That child will catch his death of cold if you don't get him home right away."

"Maybe we should," Ewen said, as Baby Thomas sneezed on cue.

I was almost ready to agree. The thought of home and sitting in front of the fire was very tempting. "Yes, we're being stupid. As if Granny Nothing would actually feed Thomas worms, and then eat him."

Just at that moment, Ewen let out a yelp of panic. Thomas was holding a wriggling worm high in the air, and his mouth was open.

I let out a yell and swiped the worm from his grubby little fingers. Thomas began to scream.

"Of course she would eat him!" I told Ewen. "The woman's a lunatic. She keeps a Shrunken Head in her case. We can't take him home. Not yet."

"We'll have to go somewhere else then. People are beginning to look at us. Probably because we should be in school."

"Or more likely because we have a baby who looks like a mud monster and who's trying to eat worms," I reminded him.

We decided to head for the hills above the town. It would be deserted there and we could walk and hide and play and no one would spot us.

I had never realized that pushing a pram up a hill could be so exhausting.

"It's about time this baby learned to walk," Ewen agreed breathlessly. Thomas only giggled.

"Can't walk. Can't talk," I muttered. "Do you think our little brother has any brains at all?"

Ewen had always doubted that. Thomas only giggled even louder. He seemed to be the only member of the family who was actually enjoying his day.

However, when we reached the top of the hill the view was worth all our efforts. It was spectacular. A rainbow stretched from somewhere in the middle of the town to the valley on the other side of the river. I tried hard to appreciate it. I'm always an optimist. But at that moment, I was too exhausted after pushing Thomas all the way to the top. Along with Ewen, I threw myself on the muddy grass and tried to get my breath back.

For one microsecond – I promise, it was only a microsecond – I took my eyes off Thomas. That baby might not be able to walk, but he was a real expert at vaulting out of his pram and crawling off. What was worse, he was on a hill. With a scream of delight, before we could grab him, he was on his way down, rolypolying all the way.

Ewen let out a bloodcurdling scream when he spotted him. So did I. We were after him in a flash. Back all the way down that dratted hill!

"I'll kill him when I catch him!" I yelled as we rushed in pursuit.

"We should have let Granny Nothing eat him!" Ewen screamed.

Thomas was practically at the bottom before we finally caught up with him. And he was still giggling.

"I've never been so exhausted in all my life!" Ewen said. He was almost crying. "Let's just go home. Please, Steph."

"There's just one little thing we've forgotten," I said softly. I was almost in tears myself.

"What?" Ewen asked, then he followed my tearful gaze back up the hill.

The baby's pram.

"I'm not going back up for it!" Ewen said.

"Neither am I!" I told him.

Thomas giggled. He didn't care who went up for it. He would be riding home in style no matter what.

"How are we going to explain the mess he's in?" Ewen said as we trudged home. We had finally drawn straws to see who would go up for the pram (well, wet grass really) and Ewen had lost. He still hadn't forgiven Thomas. Or me. He was sure I'd cheated.

"Mum and Dad will never know. They're never home till late, and we'll have him in a B-A-T-H before that." I spelled out the word in a whisper, knowing that Thomas would be out of the pram and off at warp crawling speed if he heard.

"They'll never know?" Ewen asked. "You're sure?"

"Never," I assured him.

In our dreams!

We were squelching into the kitchen when Dad suddenly yanked open the door of the living room. His face was like thunder.

"Where have you two been all day with that baby!" he yelled.

Chapter Seven

I had never seen Dad so angry. Or home so early from work.

"Where have you been?" he yelled again.

I tried to find my voice, but I couldn't. Ewen was the same. He was shaking in his Nike trainers. Thomas just giggled.

"And you!" Dad snapped at the baby. "You can shut up as well. This is no laughing matter." He began to pace the room like an angry tiger. "I get a call on my mobile right in the middle of an important meeting."

He glared at us one by one. "A VERY important meeting. Dangerfield likes my project, he really likes it! You know I've only just started in this job. You know how desperate I am to do well in it. And the call's to tell me that my children haven't come to school today. Did I know where they were? And did I?" His voice became a roar. "Did I heck! And of course, who do you think is at that meeting? Mr Dangerfield himself. Listening to every embarrassing word. Todd's in your class, Ewen. He'll be able to tell his father everything. Don't you care what my boss thinks of me?"

I almost spoke up. It was so unfair. If only he knew how much Ewen cared. I almost said something right then. But at that very second Nanny Sue appeared in the doorway. She was trying to smile, trying not to look nervous. But her chattering teeth gave her away. Dad turned his furious attention on her.

"I blame you. You're paid to take care of them. And where were you? That's what I'd like to know."

Nanny Sue had a new hairdo. New colour, new style, everything. It was obvious where she'd been.

Her face grew bright red. "I'm not taking the blame for this," she snapped back at him. "It wasn't my fault."

"Then whose fault was it?" Dad shouted.

Nanny Sue's eyes darted to me. She would have loved to have blamed me, I could see it in her venomous look, but how could she? She knew she could never admit to allowing us to take the baby for the day. Her eyes narrowed viciously. "I'll get you for this," they said to me. I smirked back.

"So. Whose fault is it?" Dad demanded again, in an even louder voice.

"Och, it was mine, son."

We all turned in shocked surprise. It was Granny Nothing, dripping in the doorway of the kitchen, soaked to the skin, like an underwater sumo wrestler.

She smiled her almost toothless grin. "I would have asked you, but the idea just came to me this morning. If I'm only going to be here for a few days, I haven't got much time to get to know the wee ones. So I thought I would take them out for the day. Och, we had a great time, didn't we, my darlin's?"

Ewen stared at her, open-mouthed.

Nanny Sue suddenly looked triumphant. "Yes. It was all her fault. She asked me, and what could I say?" Her voice all at once sounded like a little girl's. "She is your mother after all, Mr McAllister."

"I didn't think you'd mind, son."

Dad almost exploded. "Well, I do! You didn't think I'd find out, did you?" He was yelling at her. Yelling at his own mother? I was shocked.

"Of course," he went on, pacing the floor, "you wouldn't think missing a day at school's very important. You never did. If it had been up to you I'd never have gone to school at all. Well, my children are different. They are not allowed to miss school. So while you're under my roof you will obey my rules."

Granny Nothing didn't seem the least bit bothered

47

by her son's outburst. "OK, OK," she said. "Calm down. Don't burst a blood vessel."

Baby Thomas was by this time wriggling in my arms and reaching out for Granny Nothing. She stretched out her arms to him. "Come to your granny, my wee darling." She lifted him from me and the baby chuckled with joy. Even when Granny Nothing put her horrible face close to his he only giggled.

I looked at Ewen. We were both thinking the same alarming thought. Baby Thomas liked Granny Nothing. No, more than that. He loved her. Dad saw it too, and he wasn't happy about it.

"Look at the mess he's in," he snapped. "What was he doing? Rolling in the mud?"

I flushed. Got it in one, Dad.

"Shall I take him for a bath?" Nanny Sue simpered.

"Yes, indeed," Dad said.

Baby began to scream.

"Can you not see he hates baths?" Granny Nothing told him.

"I know he does," Dad said. "That's HIS punishment."

"You're a cruel boy," Granny Nothing said. "I never take a bath. Doesn't do me any harm."

So that's what the smell was, and I had been blaming poor Baby Thomas.

Nanny Sue tried to take the baby from her.

"Leave him be!" Granny Nothing roared. "I'll get him clean."

I had a sudden vision of a gorilla mother licking her baby. Was that what Granny Nothing intended for

48

Thomas? Thomas didn't seem to mind if she did. He entwined his chubby fingers round her hair and refused to let go.

Nanny Sue turned to Dad. "You know, Mr McAllister, I told her she couldn't let the children miss school. She just wouldn't listen."

What a liar!

"But she is your mother, what could I do?"

"It's not your fault, Sue," Dad said, his voice soft and forgiving. Nanny Sue had got round him once again. "I know how she can be."

This was really unfair. Poor Granny Nothing.

Poor Granny Nothing? What was I thinking? But it was true. She had stuck up for us. She had taken the blame. And here she was getting shouted at by her own son. I wanted to yell. Tell Dad the whole story. But he was already punching a number into his mobile phone. We were forgotten. He was going back to work.

Nanny Sue stepped past us. She looked smug. Smug, that is, until Granny Nothing whispered to her in her gruffest voice.

"Don't look so happy, dear, 'cause Granny Nothing is going to get you for this."

Chapter Eight

Next day at school we didn't have to tell anyone what had happened. They already knew, thanks to Todd.

"My father says you're out of control," he told us with glee. "He's going to tell your dad that. He can't have him being pulled out of important meetings to discipline his unruly children." He pushed Ewen so hard at that point he fell over. "And of course, I had to tell him about you stealing my homework jotter, and then pretending some idiot dog ate it," he went on smugly, standing over Ewen, staring down at him. "I told him

I do your homework all the time. But I told him too that I didn't want him to do anything about it. I wouldn't want your dad to lose his job."

He nudged Ewen hard with his foot and sniggered. "My dad thinks I'm wonderful."

I'd had enough of Todd Dangerfield. "You touch him one more time, and I'll thump you!"

Todd spat on to the playground, just missing Ewen by centimetres. "You do that, and I really will make sure he loses his job."

He went off laughing, so sure of himself I could have screamed.

"I wish Granny Nothing would get him!" Ewen said, remembering her threat to Nanny Sue.

"Who's Granny Nothing?" Polly asked, emerging from behind the bike sheds, warily. Polly was the littlest girl in the school, and always running from her ginger-haired tormentor, Red O'Connor, a girl who was the same age as me and as nasty as Todd Dangerfield.

Neither Ewen nor I had told any of our friends about Granny Nothing, sure she wouldn't be there long enough to matter. I hadn't wanted to talk about her. She wasn't exactly a granny you could be proud of. But now, after last night, things seemed different. She had taken the blame, and how Ewen and I had laughed as we watched her putting Baby Thomas to bed.

She had sung to him, in that gruff tuneless voice of hers, a song we had never heard before. Then she had taught it to us both.

"Who's Granny Nothing?" Polly asked again, interrupting my memory.

"She's our other granny," Ewen said, laughing. And he began to sing the song Granny Nothing had sung to us only last night.

"You cannae shove your granny off a bus,
Oh, you cannae shove your granny off a bus,
Oh, you cannae shove your granny, 'cause she's
    your mammy's mammy,
Oh, you cannae shove your granny off a bus."

I began to laugh too, as I remembered the way Granny Nothing had wobbled that belly of hers and wriggled and giggled before she began to sing the second verse.

Now, I joined in the song with my brother, "You can shove your other granny off a bus!"

And with a raucous yell Granny Nothing had shouted, "That's me! Your other granny!"

"You can shove your other granny off a bus.
You can shove your other granny, 'cause she's
    your daddy's mammy,
You can shove your other granny off a bus."

Polly loved the song. "Sing it again!" she shouted, and we did.

Soon Polly was joining in, and along with her, some of the others in the class, amazed at the display of dancing that was going on. Soon they were all singing and dancing.

"You can shove your other granny off a bus.
You can shove your other granny off a bus.
You can shove your other granny, 'cause she's
    your daddy's mammy,
You can shove your other granny off a bus."

"Can we meet her?" Polly asked as the bell rang out for classes.

I thought for only a second. Nanny Sue wouldn't like that one bit. Our friends traipsing into the house after school. "Come today," I told them all. "We'll get her to sing to you."

"Yes," Ewen told them. "She might even eat some worms."

"She doesn't eat worms," Polly said in disgust.

"You'll see," I said, and for the first time in ages, I realized I was looking forward to going home. Thanks to Granny Nothing.

But to get into the house, first we had to get past Hannibal and Lecter.

"Why are we crawling?" Polly asked in a whisper. "Is it a game?"

I nodded. I didn't want to alarm little Polly too much.

"At least there's more of us today," Ewen whispered to me. "They're bound to eat one of the others first."

He didn't whisper softly enough. "Eat! Who's going to eat who?" Polly jumped to her feet.

Her head was just slightly higher than next door's hedge. Hannibal and Lecter spotted her, almost as soon as she spotted them.

They growled.

She screamed.

Everyone else jumped to their feet. They spotted the Rottweilers. They screamed too.

Hannibal and Lecter looked at each other. They began to drool.

A feast!

They all began running at the same time. The children, and fast behind them on the other side of the garden hedge, the dogs, leaping and snarling. Eager to catch them.

Ewen made the door first. He pushed it open, held it. "Quick! Quick!" he shouted.

I was next, breathless. Then another, and another leaped through the door, falling on top of each other in the hallway, till only little Polly was left.

"Come on, Polly!" we all shouted.

Polly glanced behind her. The dogs were barking and jumping, but still on the other side of the garden.

"Don't worry, Polly." I shouted encouragement. "They can't jump the hedge."

Those dogs must have been practising. For almost at the same time, both of them did.

Polly screamed. She tried to run faster, instead she tripped and fell.

Hannibal and Lecter were right behind her. In one more second they would be on her. And there was nothing any of us could do to save her!

Grrr

Chapter Nine

"What's going on here!"

Suddenly, Granny Nothing was there, thundering down the hall like a stampeding rhinoceros. Baby Thomas was clamped under her arm. We didn't have to tell her what was going on. She took in what was happening in a second. Polly on the ground, crying. The Rottweilers leaping towards her. All the other children screaming.

She pushed Thomas into my arms. "Hold my boy!" she ordered.

Then she was off. I had never realized anyone so fat could move so fast. Yet, off she went, heading for Polly like a speeding bullet. An overweight bullet, but just as fast.

"All she has to do is fall on those dogs. She'll squash them flat," Ewen said, as he watched her.

"They'll end up like strawberry jam." I could almost picture it. "We'll have to scrape them off the path and put them in a jar."

Ewen giggled nervously.

I knew what I was expecting to happen. Any second now, Granny Nothing would scoop Polly up and race back to the house.

But she took us all by surprise.

We watched open-mouthed as she skipped over Polly Brown, and headed straight for the Rottweilers. Their eyes lit up as she came rumbling towards them. Little Polly was forgotten. She was only a snack. Here was a banquet. All that juicy flesh bouncing in their direction.

I held my breath. Granny Nothing stopped dead in front of Hannibal and Lecter. She dropped suddenly to her knees, so that her eyes were level with theirs. They stopped dead too. Taken aback. They hadn't expected this either.

In a movement so swift no one saw it coming, least of all the Rottweilers, Granny Nothing reached out and clamped her fingers round both dogs' collars.

She pulled their snarling faces close to hers. She began snarling too.

"I know who I'd be more afraid of," Ewen whispered.

Granny Nothing stared at the dogs. They stared back. She bared her teeth. They bared theirs. They growled. But Granny Nothing didn't growl back.

Instead, she threw back her head and let out an unearthly howl.

Every one of us jumped. Little Polly, still lying terrified on the path and closer than the rest of us, put her hands over her ears. Baby Thomas howled too.

Then Granny Nothing yanked the dogs even closer. So close, I was sure she was going to gobble them up. "You ever chase my children again, and do you know what?" Now she growled. The Rottweilers whimpered, struggling to be free. They'd never come across anything like Granny Nothing before. But she wasn't finished with them yet.

She let out such a roar it sent shivers down my spine. The Rottweilers whimpered even more. "Granny Nothing will get you!" she warned.

Then she threw them from her, so roughly she nearly lifted them over next door's hedge. They yelped. They whimpered. But boy, did they run. And they didn't stop till they had disappeared into the safety of their own garden.

Granny Nothing struggled to her feet and wiped her hands together. "There you are!" she said. "And that's what you tell anybody that's bad to you! Granny Nothing will get them. And so I will."

Only then did she scoop Polly up in her flabby arms.

Only then did the children begin to cheer and roar. "Granny Nothing! Yeah! Yeah! Yeah!"

On and on it went like a football chant. We clapped and cheered her inside the house still shouting, "Granny Nothing! Yeah! Yeah! Yeah!"

Granny Nothing loved it. She was beaming from one misshapen ear to the other.

"Weren't you scared?" Polly asked her.

She smiled fondly at her. "Scared? Me? Not at all. When you've grappled with tigers in India a couple of wee dogs are nothing to you."

Grappled with tigers indeed! Where would her lies end?

We all went into the kitchen and she sat at the table with Thomas bouncing on her knee. They wanted to know everything about her. Ask her questions, listen to her. Granny Nothing had never had such attention since we'd met her.

Little Polly pulled at her sleeve. "Ewen said you eat worms. You don't really do you?"

"Not at all!" she answered, then she roared with laughter. "Only on Tuesdays, Wednesdays and June. When they're in season."

"So, what do you eat on Thursdays?"

She didn't hesitate. "Creepy-crawlies," she said, licking her lips. "Oh, I can't resist a creepy-crawlie. In some countries I've visited they're quite a delicacy."

I groaned with embarrassment. Why did she have to tell such lies?

Then Granny Nothing began to sing again.

"It's cover your ears time," Ewen said, doing just that.

"Oh, I always feel so jolly when I eat a creepy-
    crawlie,
I love the way it tickles as it trickles down your
    throat.
It always makes me giggle when it starts to
    squirm and wriggle,
They're just so hard to swallow that it really gets
    your goat."

Jeremy, whose parents were in Greenpeace, was appalled. "You don't eat them alive, do you!"

Granny Nothing went on with her song, she stood up and began her wobbling dance round the table, holding a delighted Thomas high above her. Laughing, Polly joined in and wobbled as best she could.

"Then my giggling turns to gaggling and my
    energy starts flaggling,
As all the legs start scratching and I start to
    scream and shout,
Then the little devil spits."

With that she did a very realistic spit right against the wall.

"Oh, it really is the pits.
Och, they're never worth the bother so I always
    spit them out!"

Then she laughed so uproariously it was hard not to join in.

I hadn't heard so much laughing in our house for a long time.

Polly pulled at Granny Nothing's dress. "What's that dance called?" she asked.

"It's called a belly dance, sweetheart," was the answer. Granny Nothing shook and wobbled hers proudly. "And I sure have the belly for it."

Polly turned to the rest of them, giggling. "She said 'belly'." Then she put her hand over her mouth in delighted shock.

"I learned the belly dance when I was in that harem in Arabia. Oh, that sheikh just loved to see my belly dance."

Yeah, he's probably still being treated for shock.

"Goodness," Ewen whispered to me. "I'm quite proud she's my granny."

I still couldn't quite agree with that. "She's not our real granny. Our real granny's in Arizona." And no matter what Granny Nothing did she was not going to change that.

Polly was still pulling at Granny Nothing's dress. "Did you mean what you said?" she asked. "Will Granny Nothing get the bad people?"

Granny Nothing sat down and lifted Polly on to her free knee. Her other was reserved solely for Thomas. "Is there a bad one bothering you, my wee darling?"

Polly nodded. "She's called Red, 'cause she's got red hair and a bad temper. She chases me all the time. She's a bad girl."

Granny Nothing leaned close to Polly and whispered to her. "You tell her tomorrow that Granny Nothing will get her if she ever chases you again."

Ewen said in a whisper. "I wish I could threaten Todd with that." He sighed. He knew that was out of the question. Dad might lose his job if he did.

But Granny Nothing had ears like an elephant with a hearing aid.

"What was that?" she asked.

Ewen blushed. I answered for him. "Nothing, Granny Nothing."

But somehow Granny Nothing didn't look as if she believed me.

Polly was happy. "We can tell all the bad people in school tomorrow. Granny Nothing will get you."

It became another chant as Granny Nothing led them in another wobbling belly dance round the table, holding Thomas high and singing.

"Granny Nothing will get you! Granny Nothing will get you!"

I was laughing too, until I looked up and there, hiding in the doorway so no one could spot her, was Nanny Sue, clutching her new camcorder. She was watching and listening to everything with a wicked smile on her face.

Chapter Ten

"Granny Nothing will get you! What a terrible thing to say. How dare you!"

Ewen and I could distinctly hear Dad's angry voice as he stormed around the living room.

"Och, don't get your Y-fronts in a twist," came Granny Nothing's reply. "It was only a wee game." She didn't sound in the least bit apologetic. She sounded as if she was laughing. There was a definite smile in her gruff voice.

"A wee game that frightens children isn't something I can laugh about."

"She didn't frighten anyone," Ewen whispered. "Except perhaps Hannibal and Lecter."

We both giggled, remembering the Rottweilers bouncing off home, howling with fear.

Suddenly Granny Nothing's voice boomed out. "When did you become such a frozen-faced so and so? You and me used to laugh a lot together, son."

I tried hard to picture that. Dad and Granny Nothing laughing together. It just wouldn't come.

"Yes. But never at the same things," he snapped back.

"Hell's Bells and Buckets! You were never like this when you were a boy."

There was a long pause. We could hear Dad draw out a long-suffering sigh. "I will not have you frightening my children."

"It's about time you found out what they're frightened of."

"And what do you mean by that!"

But Granny Nothing was already leaving the room. The whole house began to shudder and she shouted to him. "That's for you to find out. I'm not going to interfere."

"That makes a change," Dad shouted back.

We crawled back to our rooms. "What I want to know is," I said, "who told Dad about 'Granny Nothing will get you'?"

We didn't have long to wait for an answer. Nanny Sue appeared in the doorway, smiling triumphantly. "It was a terrible thing to say," she told us. "You can't have someone like her frightening little children."

"No," Ewen said. "Not when someone like you does it so much better."

Trouble was, after meeting Granny Nothing all our friends wanted to come again, eager to see more of her. Hear her songs, watch her wobbly dance.

So after school next day, in spite of all our misgivings, we led them back to the house. No trouble from Hannibal and Lecter this time. They didn't even appear in the garden. Nanny Sue looked so disappointed as she opened the door to us.

She hugged her new camcorder to her like a pet poodle. "Such a pity," she said as we filed past her. "I thought I was going to get another good shot for my video!"

I was really mad. "You filmed that! You rat! I'm going to tell Mum on you."

She began mocking me with her sing-song voice. "She won't believe you! She won't believe you!"

"At least you won't have anything to watch tonight!" Ewen snapped.

Nanny Sue smirked. "I'll watch the repeat of the last time. Such fun. I'm going to send it in to *Video Nasties* on the telly. It's bound to be a winner. I'll be famous. And they pay you! So I'll be rich and famous."

She watched with a sneer as we all went into the kitchen where Granny Nothing was crawling on the floor with a delighted Thomas clinging to her back.

"What did she mean? About the video?" she asked me.

I told her. Granny Nothing's eyes narrowed. "Is that a

fact?" she said, then suddenly she seemed to cheer up and a big smile spread across her face.

That surprised me. I'd expected Granny Nothing to go bananas when she heard what Nanny Sue's idea of entertainment was. But of course, Granny Nothing was now the centre of attention. All our friends surrounded her, asking for songs, dances, stories.

She didn't disappoint them. But just at that moment, she had disappointed me. I'm not usually a violent person, but I suppose I had been hoping that she'd thump Nanny Sue. Nothing too violent, perhaps just tear her limb from limb. Was that too much to ask?

"Tell us a story!" Polly pleaded.

"How about the story of Miss Muffet?" Granny Nothing said.

Polly tutted. "We know about her."

Granny Nothing shook her head and told them all to be quiet. "I'm talking about the real story of Miss Muffet." She laughed and bounced Thomas on her knee.

"She was big and she was fat, and when she sat on a tuffet she squashed it flat. Oh, I knew her well."

Now they all laughed with her. She stood up, lifting Thomas high above her and started another of her wobbly dances. Then she started to sing. Well, it was meant to be singing. It sounded more as if someone had trodden on a sick cat.

"Big fat Miss Muffet sat on her tuffet,
Gobbling her curds and whey.
Along came a spider and sat down beside her,

So she ate him too.
Now the spider's inside her,
I should have said at the start of this tale,
That this Miss Muffet would never turn pale
At the sight of a spider, or even a rat.
She'd eat them all. That's why she's so fat."

The children loved it. It amazed me how much our friends loved Granny Nothing.

"You're so lucky having a granny like her. She's brilliant," Jeremy told us.

They all said the same thing.

I refused to accept that. I already had a brilliant granny. I wasn't going to betray her by suddenly preferring this one just because she could entertain our friends.

As we were all leaving Polly hung back. She looked glum.

"Now, what's the matter, sweetheart?" Granny Nothing asked her. "Did you have more trouble with that bad lassie?"

Polly blushed and nodded. "I told her you'd get her, but she said she didn't believe you really existed. She said I made you up."

"Oh, she did, did she? Well, maybe I'll just come to your school tomorrow and prove I exist, eh?"

That cheered Polly up. "Oh, will you? You promise?"

Granny Nothing crooked her little finger and beckoned Polly closer. "In fact, I'll tell ye what we'll do, honey pie."

She whispered into Polly's ear and Polly giggled. Her eyes lit up. "OK. I'll help," Polly said. And she went off in excited glee.

"You better not go to that school," Nanny Sue warned her as soon as they had all gone. "Threatening little children with your 'Granny Nothing will get you'. It's despicable."

"So, it was you that told on me?" Granny Nothing's voice was low and gruff. Like a growl. Scary.

It certainly scared Nanny Sue. She jumped back. "So! What if I did?"

Granny Nothing took another step forward and Nanny Sue fled from the kitchen.

"Aye, run!" Granny Nothing shouted after her. "Because Granny Nothing's going to get you as well."

"You can't threaten me!" Nanny Sue dared to shout back, still on the run.

Granny Nothing let out a raucous yell. "I just did, hen."

It was tea time and Granny Nothing was feeding Thomas his dinner. "Mince and Mash!" Granny Nothing was shouting. "And Granny Nothing's special ingredient."

I dreaded to think what that might be.

However, she gave Thomas his first disgusting spoonful and he seemed to love it.

At that moment Dad burst into the kitchen, closely followed by Mum and Nanny Sue. With them were our neighbours, Mr and Mrs Templeton. I was never sure which one was which. They both dressed the same, had the same haircut and talked in the same high sing-song voices.

"What did you do to our neighbours' dogs?" Dad poked a finger at Granny Nothing angrily.

"I hope I scared the life out of them. They were chasing my children."

Mrs Templeton (or was it her husband?) began to shake nervously. "Hannibal and Lecter would never chase children. Why, they're just like children themselves. And now, my poor babies won't come out from under the bed."

"Poor babies!" Granny Nothing spat the words out. "Man-eaters, more like, or children-eaters, I should say."

Mr Templeton (or was it his wife?) was quaking with anger. "Well, they're certainly not granny-eaters, are they?"

Granny Nothing grinned. "Nobody eats me and gets away with it." She sat back, ready to launch into one of her stories. "I remember once an alligator tried that up the Amazon."

Ewen's mouth fell open. "An alligator? What happened?"

Granny Nothing giggled. "Let's just say, I'm the one with the alligator handbag."

Now it was Dad who was angry. "Stop telling your lies. You've never been out of Britain and you know it."

But we'd seen the stickers, all over her case. And

we'd seen the alligator handbag, and the Shrunken Head. She couldn't be lying . . . could she?

"My poor babies are going to need doggie therapy after this."

"They *are* very scary-looking dogs, Mrs Templeton," Mum said.

"They're a couple of horrors!" I said. "Those two dogs were always after us, until Granny Nothing scared the daylights out of them."

Mrs Templeton flopped into a seat at that point with the shock. "What lies! Have you ever seen my babies chase your children, Mr McAllister?"

And of course he hadn't. I didn't point out that he was never there when we went to school, or when we came back, to catch them chasing us.

Nanny Sue pouted innocently. "You don't have to tell lies to protect your granny, Stephanie dear," she said softly. She looked at Mum. "Hannibal and Lecter look scary, but they are a couple of softies. Such darlings. I always feel safe for the children knowing they are next door."

Granny Nothing was just about to put a spoonful of mash into the baby's mouth. "What a load of mooslie!" she yelled. Thomas screamed as the spoon was yanked away from him once again.

"Well, they won't be here much longer, Nanny Sue. I'm afraid we're going to have to look for another house." Mrs Templeton's lip (I noticed there was lipstick on it, so I supposed it must have been Mrs Templeton, although with those two you could never be sure), her lip trembled with emotion. "And we plan to sell to the first weird people who make us an offer." With that she glared at Granny Nothing.

Granny Nothing glared back. "They couldn't be much weirder than you two," she said.

Ewen and I giggled. Mrs Templeton gasped with shock. Her husband, equally shocked, grasped his wife's hand and together they supported each other out of the door.

What a couple of drama queens.

"Yippee!" Granny Nothing bellowed. "Maybe now we'll get some nice neighbours."

"Nice neighbours!" Dad yelled. "You'll frighten the life out of any nice neighbours." Then he seemed to have a sudden terrifying thought. "And what do you mean . . . we. . .?"

"Och, me and this yin . . ." she made a face at Nanny Sue, "we're getting on like a house on fire. That right, dear?"

Thomas at that point grabbed her hand and tried to pull the spoon towards him.

Nanny Sue almost fainted with shock. "I can't stand you. You're driving me potty! YOU tell lies all the time."

Granny Nothing shook the spoon at Nanny Sue. Thomas began to shake his high chair in frustration. "You're the one that tells the lies, dear. Big lies."

Nanny Sue pouted innocently and looked at Dad. "Oh, Mr McAllister. You know I wouldn't do that."

Granny Nothing tutted loudly. "I'd kick that one right out of the house if I was you, son."

"I know who I'd like to kick out of the house," Dad muttered.

Baby Thomas beat the table with his fists. He was hungry. He watched the spoon with his delicious mushy mess dripping from it. Granny Nothing was waving it about all over the place, just centimetres from his open mouth.

"Your own mother! You'd kick your own mother out before her!" She sounded shocked. Hurt even. She held the spoon closer to the baby's mouth. He licked his lips, struggled to reach it. His little face was going purple.

Suddenly Granny Nothing pulled the spoon away from him, pointed it at Dad like a gun. "You've cut me to the quick, boy!" she said.

Thomas reached for the spoon. It was getting further and further away. He was ready to scream, ready to burst with frustration. And suddenly, driven to despair by hunger, he yelled at the top of his voice his very first words.

"HELL'S BELLS! AND BUCKETS!"

Chapter Eleven

Nanny Sue gasped. Mum let out a moan. Dad's jaw dropped open. Baby Thomas yelled again at the top of his voice. "Hell's! Bells!"

Granny Nothing wiped a sentimental tear from the corner of her eye. "The wee soul has said his first words at last." She looked at Dad. "Thanks to me."

If she expected him to be grateful she was in for a shock. Now it was Dad's turn to go purple.

"Thanks to you my son's first words are swear words."

Granny Nothing shrugged her shoulders innocently. Baby Thomas yelled again and beat the table with his chubby fists. "Hell's! Bells! Hell's! Bells!"

"Will you keep quiet!" Dad shouted at him.

But now that he'd started talking he didn't want to stop.

"Well, Dad," Ewen said. "You did always want him to talk, didn't you?"

Mum picked the baby up. She looked near to tears. Thomas struggled in her arms. He'd never done that before. He'd always been too glad to be taken away from Nanny Sue. But now that Granny Nothing was here, she was all he wanted. No one else would do. Finally, Mum gave up. She handed the baby over. But she wasn't happy about it. "You've even turned my baby against me," she said, and she fled from the kitchen almost in tears.

"You've taught my son to swear," Dad said, and before he hurried after Mum he added, "You were always causing trouble when I was a boy, and you're still causing trouble. The sooner you're out of here the better." He glared at her.

Nanny Sue smirked. "I second that." But she waited till Dad had left the room before she said it.

"I bet you'll be going before me," Granny Nothing said, as if she knew something Nanny Sue didn't. Nanny Sue wasn't bothered now by her threats. She was sure she held the upper hand. Mum and Dad preferred her, obviously.

It was only when Nanny Sue had left the room that

Granny Nothing seemed to deflate, like a barrage balloon with a leak. For the first time since we'd known her she looked genuinely hurt. "I think I'm in trouble."

Ewen sat beside her, putting his hand on her arm to comfort her. "Dad shouts at you all the time. He doesn't mean it." All the same, he wasn't sure this time that it was true.

Granny Nothing shook her head. "No. He doesn't like his old mother. I don't think he ever did."

"Why doesn't he love you?" I dared to ask.

Granny Nothing just shrugged. "I don't know. I mean, I'm a loveable kind of person, don't you think?"

She didn't wait for an answer. She just assumed we would agree with that. "But I'm not very ladylike, I suppose. And I can be a bit loud. I've always embarrassed him. Maybe if I took elocution lessons . . . what do you think?"

"Have you really been to all those countries?" I asked her. "Done all those things?"

She rolled her eyes and nodded. "Oh aye. Your granny's done many strange and wonderful things. I'll tell ye about them one day."

And I remembered the Shrunken Head, and shivered.

But if Dad didn't love her, Baby Thomas made up for him with the affection he lavished on her. Already, he was clambering all over her, pulling her hair, kissing her, and by the time we went to bed Granny Nothing was back to her old self, laughing and kissing him back.

"Imagine Granny Nothing kissing you," Ewen said with a shudder as we sat on the bus to school next day.

"I'd never allow it." The very idea made me feel sick. "I'm sure I'd catch something."

Ewen hesitated. "Still, I don't think Dad should send her away, do you?"

I didn't even have to think about it. I still thought caring about her was betraying Granny Fielding. "Wouldn't bother me at all. She has to go sometime. The sooner the better."

I knew I didn't really mean that. I even had a funny feeling I might miss her.

I was hurrying out of the school gates at three o'clock and there she was, with Baby Thomas tucked underneath her arm.

Why doesn't she ever put him in his pram? I thought in annoyance. She always holds him as if he were a baby gorilla. Then I shrugged. In my opinion my little brother resembled a baby gorilla anyway.

"What are you doing here?" I demanded, sounding more like Dad than I meant to. Granny Nothing's eyes scoured the playground behind me. "I'm waiting for someone," she said.

Suddenly, Polly was racing towards us, screaming and shouting and breathless. Chasing her was Red, her flaming hair flying behind her. Yet, it seemed to me as

I watched that Red wasn't so much chasing Polly, as being led by her. Led straight into the jaws of Granny Nothing. And I remembered the whispers and the plans and Polly's gleeful "I'll help".

Polly ran right behind Granny Nothing and hid herself in the folds of her massive body. Red stopped dead. She looked up, centimetre by centimetre, at Granny Nothing's looming figure. Even with a gurgling baby under her arm, she was a terrifying sight. Like a mother gorilla whose baby has been threatened.

"I'm Granny Nothing," she said. I had never heard her voice sound so gruff. I expected to see nails fire from her mouth any second. "And I don't like BAD girls. Do you hear me?"

Red tried to look tough and hard. Usually that was easy for her, but not now. Granny Nothing bent down so she could look straight into Red's eyes. Red swallowed nervously.

"Granny Nothing doesn't like BAD girls. Understand? And Granny Nothing will get you if you ever chase this wee lassie again."

Red looked at Polly. She swallowed again. She looked back at Granny Nothing. Then her nervous eyes glanced once more at Polly. Why, she almost smiled. Then, she turned and ran. I had a funny feeling that Polly wouldn't be having any more trouble from that quarter, thanks to Granny Nothing.

Polly threw her arms around her. "Oh thank you. And I promise. I'll always be a good girl."

And Polly turned and walked off home. And for the first time she didn't run, or look behind her, or seem scared.

"How could anybody hurt that wee darling?" Granny Nothing said, gazing after her fondly. Then she looked all around the empty playground. "What's keeping Ewen?"

What WAS keeping my brother? A warning bell sounded in my head. It was as if Granny Nothing could hear it too.

"Here!" She pushed Thomas into my arms. "You hold my boy." And before I could protest she was off, lumbering into the playground.

"Do you think we should wait here?" I suggested to Thomas.

He mumbled something. It could have been, "Not on your nelly!"

I had to agree. "Come on. We're going after her."

We caught up with her just as she was going round the corner at the bike sheds.

I let out a scream. There was Ewen, lying on the ground, held down by two of Todd's friends. Ewen's nose was bleeding, and there too, standing over him arrogantly, was Todd Dangerfield. His fist was raised, and he was ready to pound into Ewen's face once again!

Chapter Twelve

"Hell's Bells and Buckets! What's going on here?"

Todd Dangerfield turned at the sound of Granny Nothing's booming voice. His jaw almost hit the playground.

"What is that!"

Granny Nothing went charging towards him. "If you've hurt my boy you're going to be very sorry, son."

The two boys who were holding Ewen down took one look at the charging rhinoceros heading for them, and ran.

"Come back, you cowards!" Todd shouted after them. For a second he looked as if he was ready to run too, then his shoulders straightened. He stood tall. He had remembered who he was. His father was Ewen's father's boss, after all.

"I think you'd better get out of here," he said with assurance.

"Me?" Granny Nothing said, reaching out for him. "I'm going nowhere. And neither are you." She grabbed him by the collar and almost lifted him off his feet. She looked at Ewen. "Get up, son. It's a fair fight now. One against one."

Ewen rose unsteadily to his feet. He sniffed and swallowed some blood. He looked at Granny Nothing. Then at Todd. Then his eyes went back to Granny Nothing. He lowered his eyes sheepishly. "Just let him go. Just leave it be."

Granny looked puzzled. "What!"

Todd struggled to be free of her. "Yes. Let me go, you silly old boot."

Granny was still looking at Ewen. "What's going on here, Ewen, son?"

"He doesn't dare hit me," Todd told her with a sneer. "He knows what's good for him . . . and he'd better tell you too. Now, let – me – go!" He began to squirm and shake, but Granny Nothing would not release her hold on him.

"Let me go!" Todd screamed at her. "Or you're the one who'll be sorry."

Granny Nothing laughed. "Son. I've met worms that scared me more than you."

I watched as Todd's face went white with rage. What was he going to do? Suddenly, he lifted his foot and began kicking Granny Nothing hard on the shins.

She let out a yelp, but she still didn't let him go. "You wee—"

Todd kicked her even harder.

Suddenly, there was a scream and a yell, this time from Ewen. "You leave my granny be!" Ewen ran at Todd. Only then did Granny Nothing let him go. Todd staggered back. Ewen ran right into him and they both tumbled to the ground, locked together.

Granny Nothing jumped about with delight. "That's a good one, son!" She obviously loved a good fight. "Stand up for yourself." She was throwing imaginary punches, left and right. She danced round the two boys and her body seemed to ripple every time she moved. "This takes me back to my time as a sumo wrestler in Japan. Aw, happy days."

I gasped. What a liar! She was never a sumo wrestler. She couldn't have been . . . could she? The thought of her great bare buttocks wobbling about was too horrible to imagine.

She yelled words of encouragement to Ewen, like a coach at a wrestling match. Not that Ewen needed any encouragement. Now that he was on his feet, in a fair fight, he was full of energy. Todd Dangerfield had bullied him for so long and he'd done nothing about it. Boy, was he making up for it now! Todd didn't stand a chance. He could only fight with two of his friends holding Ewen down. On his own, he was useless. One of Ewen's punches hit home, right on the nose. And suddenly, it was Todd who was covered in blood. He grabbed at his nose. "You've broken it!" he yelled. "I'll get you for this." He looked at Granny Nothing with hate in his eyes. "I'll get both of you." Then he ran off, staggering across the playground, blood dripping everywhere.

Granny Nothing was laughing. "There! I bet he won't give you any trouble again." She grabbed Thomas from me and threw him in the air. Thomas responded as ever with an over-excited giggle.

"Come on my wee cuddly bundle of joy. Home for tea . . . and a big plate of. . ." Now Granny Nothing was giggling. "Wurums!"

Ewen lifted his torn jacket and trailed forlornly behind her. He looked at me, a worried frown on his face. "What have I done, Steph?"

We were soon to know.

Chapter Thirteen

It was a horrible night. After tea Nanny Sue sat in the kitchen, warbling some pop song. She was so out of tune it was impossible to recognize what it was. She had been singing since we came home. At least she was happy. Granny Nothing was in the bedroom with Thomas, playing racing cars, and their excited "vroom-vrooms" could be heard all through the house. Mum was still working but Dad was home for once, concentrating hard on his new project for Dangerfield Electronics. He sat at the table with his charts and graphs spread out before him. He hadn't even noticed the beginnings of Ewen's black eye. Nanny Sue had, but she'd only commented that it was an improvement. We had sworn Granny Nothing to secrecy about what had happened today.

But Ewen and I were worried. A sense of impending doom hung over us. As if we were just waiting for the guillotine to fall.

We both jumped when the phone rang. I held my breath as I heard Nanny Sue clip into the hall and lift the receiver.

"Can I ask who's calling?" we heard her ask, in her prim telephone voice. Then she clipped into the living room. "It's for you, Mr McAllister. Mr Dangerfield."

Dad jumped to his feet. "He'll be wanting to know how the project's going." And he hurried to the phone.

I felt Ewen tense beside me. His face went chalk white.

"Maybe it's nothing to do with what happened," he said, trying to make himself feel better. "Maybe Mr Dangerfield didn't notice Todd's broken nose."

"He'd be hardly likely to miss that."

"Dad missed my black eye," Ewen reminded me.

We were ready to listen at the door, but just then Mum came in and slapped her briefcase down on the table. "I'm sick to death of trying to talk to stupid people who just won't listen!"

Nanny Sue came into the living room right at that moment and switched on the television. *Star-Maker* was just about to come on and she just couldn't miss that.

She looked smug and she was still singing. To add to the din, Granny Nothing roared in with Thomas on her back. She was screeching like a hyena and Thomas was screaming with excitement. At that same moment Mum's mobile began to ring.

"It's a madhouse in here!" she shouted.

And all Ewen and I could think was, *what is happening on that phone!*

We didn't have long to find out.

Suddenly Dad exploded into the room. He almost had the door off its hinges in his anger.

"Shut up all of you!" He screamed the words out.

Mum switched off her phone. Nanny Sue switched off the television. Granny Nothing shut her mouth. And even Baby Thomas stopped screaming.

The silence was ominous.

Dad looked all around the room. His angry gaze rested on Ewen. "That was Mr Dangerfield on the phone. He tells me that you, Ewen, have been bullying his son, Todd, for ages. Todd hasn't told his father because he didn't want to jeopardize my new job."

Ewen and I both were so gobsmacked, we couldn't say a word.

Dad turned his attention to Granny Nothing. "And today, you held Todd Dangerfield down so my son could punch lumps out of him!"

Ewen at last found his voice. "But Dad. . ." he began to protest.

Dad wouldn't listen. "I don't want to hear another word," he yelled. "And as for you!" He jabbed a furious finger at his mother. "I want you out of this house immediately. There's been nothing but trouble since you came here. And now, because of you –" he looked around us all – "I've just been fired."

Chapter Fourteen

Dad stormed out of the living room, too angry to say another word.

Mum yelled at Granny Nothing. "It's all your fault! He's worked so hard at this job. Wanted to make a success of it. He was always so ashamed of the life he had with you. And now, he's lost that job. And all because of you." Then she too rushed from the room.

Granny Nothing stood silently, staring at the floor. Baby Thomas gurgled in her arms, dribbling all down her. She didn't say a word for a long time.

I wondered what she was thinking. Did she believe Ewen really had been bullying Todd? And that today Todd had only been trying to get his own back? "Granny Nothing will get you if you're bad."

Would she really think Ewen had been the one who'd been bad?

I held my breath as Granny Nothing raised her eyes at last. She fixed them on Ewen, and then she shook her head.

Ewen began to protest "But I . . . it wasn't . . . I mean. . ."

Still she shook her head, and then she said softly. "So, that's why you wouldn't fight back. Because you didn't want your daddy to lose his job."

Ewen nodded.

"And how long has this been going on?"

I answered her. "Ever since Dad got the job, Todd's been picking on Ewen. It's been awful for him."

"Och, my poor wee man," and she held out her free arm to Ewen.

He didn't hesitate. He ran to her and was enveloped in all her flabby flesh.

"I shouldn't have fought with him," he mumbled. "I knew this would happen."

I was sure my brother was crying. Either that or he was being suffocated. It was hard to tell.

"You only fought with him when he started kicking me. You were sticking up for your old granny." She ruffled his hair with her chubby chip fingers. "You're the bravest boy I've ever come across."

"Much Dad cares!" I snapped.

"Aye, well, I'll be telling him the whole story, don't you worry."

"He won't listen. He never listens," Ewen mumbled.

"He will this time," Granny Nothing said with assurance. "And let's look on the bright side. At least the night can't get any worse."

How wrong can you be?

Ten minutes later the headmaster, Mr Bassett, arrived at the door. His face was flushed and angry. Even his bald head was bright red. He didn't even say hello as he barged into the house.

"Where are your father and mother, Stephanie?" he demanded. "Get them for me at once."

"And who the dickens are you!" Granny Nothing asked cheekily, coming in from the kitchen with Baby Thomas still attached to her like Velcro.

Mr Bassett didn't answer her. For a moment he was too shocked to answer. His mouth fell open and his eyes popped. "No need to ask who you are. You have to be the famous Granny Nothing."

Granny Nothing looked dead pleased. "Oh, famous am I?"

"Perhaps 'notorious' might be a better word."

I wasn't one hundred per cent sure what notorious meant, but I had a feeling it wasn't half as complimentary as "famous".

"And why should she be 'notorious', Mr Bassett?" This was Dad, who had just come downstairs.

Mum was right behind him. "What's she done now?" She snatched Thomas from Granny Nothing's arms and he immediately began to wail.

I suddenly realized they were all against Granny Nothing, and she had done absolutely nothing wrong. It just wasn't fair. "She hasn't done anything!" I shouted, moving to Granny Nothing's side.

"Hasn't she?" Mr Bassett tried not to shout, but he didn't quite manage it. "I've had a string of phone calls this evening, parents protesting about this bizarre –" he chose his next word carefully – "creaturrre," he said at last. Rolling the R around his tongue until he finally spat it out. "She has been frightening little children."

Granny Nothing looked affronted. "Me? Frighten a child? Never!"

She wobbled all over with indignation.

"Yes, frightening them. Red O'Connor has been hiding under the bed since she came home from school. Sure you're coming to get her. And as for little Todd Dangerfield. . ."

I looked at Ewen in amazement. Todd? Little? He was the tallest boy in the school. Baldy Bassett only came up to Todd's shoulders. "Little Todd says there has been a vendetta against him and that YOU –" he poked a finger at Granny Nothing – "helped this horrible child –" the finger moved to Ewen – "to beat Todd to a pulp today."

"That's not true. None of it's true!" Ewen shouted.

"You didn't punch him on the nose?" Mr Bassett demanded.

"Well, yes," Ewen had to admit.

"And YOU didn't have him dangling by the collar?" Mr Bassett asked of Granny Nothing.

"No doubt about that," she said proudly.

"I rest my case," Mr Bassett said, like an idiot. He didn't even have a case with him.

"But not at the same time," Ewen tried to explain. But no one would listen. Why did grown-ups never listen?

Granny Nothing took a step forward. "I've got a few words to say about this."

She didn't get any further. Dad interrupted her. "You have nothing more to say here. Since you came to this house there has been nothing but trouble. Our neighbours are moving out, I've lost my job, and you've turned our children against us."

"My son's first words were swear words," Mum said trying to hold back tears. "I insisted we take you in because I thought your son must be exaggerating about you. I see now he wasn't. You're every bit as bad as he told me you were!"

"You were the worst mother any boy could ever have," Dad said. It was the cruellest thing I had ever heard my dad say. The cruellest thing any son could say to his mother.

Granny Nothing felt it. She seemed to sag, as if the air was going out of a balloon. And still Dad wasn't finished. "I won't let you be the worst grandmother. I want you out of this house. And I never want you to come back. I never want my children to see you again."

We were too shocked to say a word. Maybe Granny Nothing was too, because she just bent her head and slumped out of the room. She even ignored Thomas's outstretched arms and his sudden yell of "Hell's Bells and Buckets!"

The door had closed behind her before I had the nerve to say a word.

"That's not fair. That's just not fair. Nothing was her fault. Nothing!"

But no one wanted to listen. Not Mr Bassett, who began to berate Ewen about his treatment of "little" Todd. Not Dad, who began to give us both a lecture about bullying. Mum seemed our only hope. She was quiet and close to tears, trying to get Thomas to stop screaming.

"Mum, please listen to us. . ." Ewen pleaded.

"I'm too upset, Ewen," was all she said. "We'll talk in the morning. But I do have some good news." She tried to smile but couldn't. "I phoned Granny Fielding. And she's coming back." Suddenly, she started to sob against her wailing baby. "I need to see my mother," she cried.

Granny Fielding was coming. Wonderful Granny Fielding. She'd know what to do. She'd sort everything out. I felt better immediately.

When we were finally allowed to go to bed we both made a beeline for the room Granny Nothing had been sharing with Nanny Sue. Ewen knocked softly.

"Granny Nothing, can we come in?"

There was no reply.

"Maybe she's sleeping," Ewen said. But there was no snoring coming from the room so we knew that was hardly likely.

I knocked loudly. "Please, can we come in?"

There was still no answer.

I turned the handle of the door and pushed it open. I looked all around the room. Her bed hadn't been slept in. The old battered case she had arrived with wasn't underneath her sofa bed any more.

Granny Nothing had gone!

Chapter Fifteen

We ran downstairs in a panic. Dad and Mum and a wailing Thomas were showing Mr Bassett out. Dad's face did not betray any kind of emotion. He simply said softly, "So, that's it then."

Mr Bassett beamed with delight. "She's gone? Oh, that's wonderful. I'll phone Mr Dangerfield tonight. He said poor Todd was frightened to come to school tomorrow." At that his smile became a glare directed at Ewen. "But now that SHE'S gone there's nothing to be frightened of."

"Not for the bullies anyway," I felt like telling him.

Mr Bassett went down the path practically singing, he was so happy.

"What are we going to do about Granny Nothing, Dad?" I demanded as Dad closed the door.

He shrugged his shoulders. "She's perfectly capable of taking care of herself."

"But where will she sleep?" Ewen asked, imagining her walking the streets with her old battered suitcase, frightening the life out of some poor homeless man as she threw him out of a doorway and took his place.

"In a hotel probably," Dad answered curtly. "I don't care. I have enough on my mind tonight." He looked at us both. "And you two get to bed. I'll speak to you in the morning." He paused. "I'll listen in the morning." He said it as if he meant it. Then he turned his gaze on Thomas, still screeching at the top of his voice. "Can no one shut that baby up!"

Only Granny Nothing, I thought wearily as I climbed the stairs to bed.

"Do you think she'll ever come back?" I asked Mum when she came into my room to turn out the light.

"I hope not!" she said at once. And Thomas, held in her arms, wailed even louder.

He still hadn't stopped next morning when I came down for breakfast. Nanny Sue was screeching out a song as she boiled the eggs. She'd won. She was still here, and Granny Nothing, her arch-enemy, was gone. Thomas was perched on Dad's knee. The baby's eyes were red, his nose was running, his chubby little fingers were pounding on the table. Poor Thomas. Dad was doing everything he could to pacify the baby, but nothing worked. He only wanted one thing. He wanted Granny Nothing. And that only made Dad furious.

"If you got Granny Nothing back, Thomas would soon shut up," Ewen said hopefully.

"I'd rather have a wailing baby than her back in my house," Dad snapped at him. "Anyway, I'll be able to stay at home and look after him now that I don't have a job any more." He glared at Ewen. "Isn't that lucky."

Nanny Sue pranced into the kitchen. "I'll take care of Thomas, Mr McAllister. I have ways of making him quiet."

Yes, I thought, *chloroform springs to mind.*

"You'll get another job, Dad," Ewen promised him.

"Will I?" Dad didn't sound too hopeful. "It took me long enough to get this one."

Mum bustled into the kitchen stuffing papers into her briefcase. "Don't listen to him. Dad will soon be back at work." She looked at Dad. "Haven't you told them yet?"

"Told us what?" Yet my stomach began to churn as if it knew what he had to tell us wouldn't be good.

Dad took a deep breath. "I've been on the phone to Mr Dangerfield. He's willing to give me my job back."

"Oh Dad, that's wonderful!" Ewen said. He had hardly slept all night because he'd been feeling so guilty about everything.

"On one condition." Dad looked directly into Ewen's eyes. "That you apologize to Todd, and promise that you'll never do it again."

Ewen stared back at him. His mouth hung open.

"Why are you looking so shocked?" Dad snapped. "Is it so hard to apologize? Don't you want me to get my job back? You were the one doing the bullying, weren't you?" He waited for an answer. Was this the moment to tell him the truth? Or didn't he want the truth if the truth meant he would never get his job back? Maybe he was disappointed that Ewen didn't say anything then. He just stared down at the floor, looking guilty. Dad let out a long sigh, and said, "I see. In that case, I think it was very good of Todd not to tell his father for so long."

I was shocked into silence too. After everything that Ewen had come through, he was going to have to apologize to Todd Dangerfield. And it would all begin again. Ewen's life a misery, and Todd even more powerful than ever. It just wasn't fair!

Ewen's face flushed. He was almost ready to cry. I felt like hugging him. Hug my brother? That was a first.

"I suppose if it means you get your job back."

"Fine. I'll come over to the school later. Mr Dangerfield says you can apologize in the headmaster's office. He'll be there with Todd and I'll be there with you."

Ewen just stared. "You mean I've to apologize in front of him?" This was even worse than he had imagined.

"I think it was good of Mr Dangerfield not to insist

you do it in front of the whole school. I think I might have insisted on that."

I wanted to scream at him. It was so unfair. What would Granny Nothing do? But Granny Nothing wasn't here. We had no one on our side now.

"It will be worth it in the end, isn't that right, Ewen darling?"

This was Nanny Sue, simpering. Dad was, as usual, totally taken in. "Thank you, Nanny Sue."

We all went with Mum to the front door to see her off. She kissed Dad and pulled the door open. "What's this?" she said, and she picked up a parcel which was lying on the steps. "It's addressed to you." She handed the parcel to Dad. It was wrapped untidily in brown paper. "I think it's from your mother."

We all moved back into the living room. Dad seemed reluctant to open it. He drummed his fingers on it for a while, just looking at it.

"Maybe it's a bomb," Nanny Sue said, pretending to polish the table.

"Oh, open it, I'm dying to know what's inside." Mum put down her briefcase and waited. Nanny Sue reluctantly went back into the kitchen.

Slowly, Dad unravelled the parcel. Inside, to our surprise, was a video tape, and attached to it a note. Dad didn't read the note at once. He stood up and deposited Thomas in Mum's arms. He stooped down to the video machine and slid the tape in. "Maybe it's a last-ditch confession of all her wrongs," he said.

Ewen began to get scared. "Maybe it's a suicide tape.

She wouldn't have left a note. She wasn't very good at writing."

Dad waved the note that had been attached to the tape. "Well, she bothered to write something this time." He flopped down on the sofa. "This should be interesting." He flicked the switch of the video.

The video crackled and jumped and then, suddenly, Ewen and I appeared, running up the path to our front door, terror etched on our faces.

"What's this!" All at once, Dad was interested. He sat up straight.

Behind us on the video, all our friends were running too, looking every bit as frightened as we were. And, on the other side of the fence, Hannibal and Lecter could be clearly heard, barking, growling . . . hungry. Suddenly, Little Polly came into view. She was panting and running as fast as her little legs could carry her. She glanced behind her just as Hannibal and Lecter jumped the fence. That was just too much for Little Polly. She let out a terrified scream as she tripped and fell headlong along the path with the hounds of hell closing in.

Mum gasped. "Who was taking this film? Why didn't they help? Do they call this entertainment!"

Just then there was a little giggle. It came from someone behind the camera. Someone who was finding it all very amusing. Ewen and I exchanged glances.

"They were laughing." Dad was shocked. "If I ever find out who that was. . ."

At that very moment Nanny Sue tripped into the living room. She took in all the shocked faces, and then the video and her simpering smile became a look of utter shock. It was worth a million pounds to see it.

"Oh dear, that's awful. Put that off, you'll frighten the children." She reached out to take the remote control from Dad, but he pulled it away from her.

"Do you know anything about this, Nanny Sue?" And before she could say a word he added, "If I thought my mother was taking videos like this. . ."

I almost yelled. Typical. Blame Granny Nothing for everything.

Nanny Sue couldn't resist. "Yes. It was her. I tried to stop her. But you know what she was like."

Her voice trailed off, for just at that very moment, Granny Nothing lumbered on to the screen. Down the path she went, heading for Polly. Heading for the Rottweilers. Dad drew in his breath as she grabbed the dogs by the collars. He gasped as she dragged their faces close to hers and scared the living daylights out of them. He watched in total amazement as the dogs turned with their tails actually between their legs and whined their way back into their own garden. This time, he was gobsmacked, lost for words. In the video, we all cheered and chanted as Granny Nothing swept little Polly up in her arms and hugged her. And then, just as Granny Nothing was heading back to the house, the whining voice of a very disappointed Nanny Sue could be distinctly heard.

"Trust her to spoil my entertainment again! I hate that old woman!"

Mum turned to Nanny Sue. Dad turned to Nanny Sue. They were looking at her as if she'd just been turned into a three-headed monster.

"How could you?" Mum said.

Now, for once, Nanny Sue was lost for words. "It was an accident. I . . . I was just trying out my new camcorder, and it happened. So I caught it on camera. I thought I might send it in to *Video Nasties* . . . if I'd got it on TV I was going to take you all on holiday with the money. . ." she finished weakly. No one believed her.

Mum screamed at her. She almost leaped across the table. "I'll get you for this!" she yelled.

Nanny Sue took a step back, lost her balance and landed on the floor, just as Thomas tipped his bowl of cold porridge all over her face. Now, SHE began to wail.

I couldn't resist bending down and saying to Nanny Sue. "You were right. It was a bomb!"

I beamed at Ewen and he beamed back. Nanny Sue had been found out at last. Thanks to Granny Nothing! And she wasn't even here.

Chapter Sixteen

Dad was opening the note that Granny Nothing had left. He read it to himself. It seemed ages before he handed it to Mum and we both crowded round.

Now you know the kind of person you've trusted to look after your children. I'm not there to protect them now. So I'm relying on you to get rid of that monster. They never told you about her because they knew how hard your working. They didn't want to worry you. They're the best children any body could ever have. So listen to them. I mite have been the worstest mother in the world. But I always listened. And I always took your side.

"She spells 'might' m-i-t-e," was all he said.

He looked deflated. So did Mum. She sat beside him and put her arm around his shoulders.

Granny Nothing wasn't here, but she was still protecting us. Well, I wasn't going to let her down. I knew now exactly what I was going to do.

I looked at Ewen. "You are not going to apologize to Todd Dangerfield," I said flatly.

Dad turned round. "What did you say?"

I stood my ground. "I said, Ewen is not going to apologize to Todd Dangerfield." I had never spoken like that to Dad, but I wasn't going to stop now. "You're going to do exactly what Granny Nothing told you. For once, you're going to keep quiet and listen."

Mum's mouth hung open. Even Baby Thomas shut up. Nanny Sue and her porridge-covered face took the opportunity to crawl back into the kitchen.

I was more confident now. "Todd Dangerfield is a nasty, horrible boy who's been picking on Ewen ever since you got that job. He threatened to get you fired if Ewen ever said anything. So Ewen didn't. He put up with every disgusting, horrible thing Todd did, just so you could keep your rotten job. Just the way we put up with Nanny Sue. And yesterday, when Todd's mates were holding Ewen down so Todd could kick the daylights out of him, Ewen still wouldn't fight back, because of you." I took a deep breath before I went on, "And that's when Granny Nothing appeared. She stepped in and saved Ewen. And it was only when Todd Dangerfield started kicking lumps out of Granny Nothing that Ewen fought back. To protect his granny."

Now, Ewen joined in. "And as for Nanny Sue, if you don't get rid of her now, I'll leave home. She's horrible and nasty, and she doesn't treat Baby Thomas right at all. But you were both too busy to see that. Granny Nothing came and she saw it right away. She protected us from her. But now, you've got rid of her. She was the only friend we had, the only one who helped us. She helped us at home. And she helped us at school. She even stopped next door's Rottweilers from trying to eat us every day."

He ran for the door almost as if our parents were going to chase him. "And I won't apologize to Todd Dangerfield. Not for you or anybody else."

I ran all the way to school. With Ewen streaks ahead of me. I was worried about him. He was upset. But so was I. I was frightened too. What was it going to be like at school?

It was worse than I could ever have imagined.

Little Polly was hiding in the bike sheds from Red O'Connor. "Where are you, Polly?" she was shouting. "Granny Nothing can't save you now. She's gone. It's all over the school. No more Granny Nothing."

Then Todd Dangerfield appeared from behind the bike sheds and joined in her chant. "No More Granny Nothing! No More Granny Nothing!"

Soon every bully in the school had joined in the chant. "No More Granny Nothing!"

Little Polly raced from the bike sheds straight into my arms. She was almost in tears. "We've got to get her back, Steph. We've just got to get her back."

She was right. I knew that. But how? We didn't know where she'd gone. How would we ever find her?

Chapter Seventeen

"I know what we'll do!" Ewen said suddenly. "We'll have a sit-down strike."

I was puzzled. "Sit down . . . where?" I asked him.

"In the playground. Right here."

He pointed to the damp ground.

"What if it rains?" I asked.

"If I get my knickers wet my mum will really get mad," Polly moaned.

"Oh shut up about your knickers!" Ewen said. He thought it was a great idea. "And it won't rain."

"So how is a sit-down strike going to help us get back Granny Nothing?" All I could see it getting us was cold bottoms.

"Because before we start you're going to phone the local paper. Get a reporter and a photographer round here. We'll make the front page. Granny Nothing will see it. She'll see how much we need her. She'll have to come back then."

Polly's eyes were filled with admiration as she looked up at Ewen. "That's brilliant."

"I thought so, too," he said.

"And why have I got to phone the paper?" I complained.

"Because you sound so grown-up on the phone. You've got a lovely telephone voice."

Well, that was true, I thought. I just had never thought that Ewen agreed. "Are you taking the mickey?"

He gave me a push. "Better hurry. The bell will be going in five minutes."

I dashed off to the phone box at the corner. and found I had to look up the number of the local paper. Then, when I finally did get through they put me on hold for ages listening to Robbie Williams. I was ready to scream down the phone before a reporter finally came on the line.

"A sit-down strike?" the reporter asked. "In a primary school?" She sounded as if she was ready to laugh.

"We're protesting," I said, already getting a bit annoyed by her attitude.

"What about?"

"You'll find that out when you come. Oh, and bring a photographer," I said, before she hung up.

"A photographer?" The reporter sounded incredulous now.

"Well, you wouldn't want to miss little children being dragged into school by the hair, would you?"

That picture seemed to catch her interest and when I ran back to the playground I was able to tell Ewen with some assurance. "They'll be here."

Luckily, the bell was late that morning. After all, Mr Bassett had had a hard night pacifying all the bullies' parents.

Finally, however, it rang and we all lined up ready to file inside.

Mr Bassett arrived, his bald head shining as a shaft of sunlight caught it.

"Everybody inside, children," he said, clapping his hands.

On cue, exactly as we had decided, the pupils sat down on the ground. Mr Bassett's eyes almost popped out. "What's going on here?" he demanded, his eyes heading straight for me, as if I had to be the ringleader.

"It's a protest, sir," I said. "A sit-down strike."

"What on earth for?" he yelled.

Polly tried to speak, but I told her to be quiet. "We'll tell you when the press arrive."

"The press? You're expecting the press?" Mr Bassett was fast heading for a collapse. He looked around at his teachers. "Get these children inside," he yelled at them.

But they only shrugged. "And how do we do that?"

"Drag them in." Mr Bassett was losing his temper.

"That won't look too good if the papers do come."

Mr Bassett stamped his feet like a schoolboy. "Get inside this school . . . NOW!"

The only ones who obeyed him, and this made a real change, were Red and her friends, and Todd Dangerfield and his gang. He looked at them affectionately. "Like these model pupils," he said.

"Model pupils! Ha!" Ewen shouted.

Todd Dangerfield was smirking. "I told you Ewen McAllister was a troublemaker, sir," he said, grinning.

"I see that now, Todd. Right. I'm phoning your parents. They'll soon get you on the move." And off he went marching inside the school to his office.

The parents arrived just about the time the reporter and the photographer did. And that included Todd Dangerfield's dad, who had turned up for Ewen's apology. Our dad arrived about the same time. Baby Thomas was still clutched in his arms.

"What's the idea of this, Steph?" he asked.

"We want Granny Nothing back," Ewen said simply. "And we don't intend to move until you find her."

"Who is Granny Nothing?" the reporter asked, already scribbling in her notebook.

"She's the scariest granny in the world," Polly said with a giggle.

"She's been frightening the children," Mr Bassett told her, making sure she was spelling his name correctly.

"Only the bad ones," Ewen corrected.

109

"The bullies!"

"Granny Nothing loves me," said little Polly. "Because I'm good. She doesn't scare good girls or boys."

"She scares me," Todd Dangerfield shouted. His friends all called out in agreement.

"And me," Red said. "She's scary, Granny Nothing."

"That's because you're bad. You've been picking on me for ages." Polly didn't sound the least bit scared of Red now. "And Granny Nothing told you she'd get you if you were bad to me again. That's why she scares you."

Red's face had gone the same colour as her hair. "I'll get you for that, you little horror." Then she realized what she'd said and looked sheepishly round the assembled parents and teachers. "Or I would. If I was really bad. . ."

"And why are you scared of Granny Nothing, Todd?" Dad asked.

"Because she's not a very nice person. She's ugly. She looks like a big, fat elephant, and she smells. Yuch!" He laughed. His friends laughed too. He didn't seem to notice that no one else did.

"It couldn't be because you're not a very nice person, could it, Todd? Because you've been bullying my son for months and threatening to get me fired if he told on you?"

I looked at Ewen. Dad believed us! At last, he really did believe us.

Mr Dangerfield put an arm around his son. "If you want your job back, McAllister, you're going the wrong way about it."

"Maybe I'd rather not have a job, if it means my son's whole life being made a misery."

A cheer went up. Dad smiled, first at Ewen, then at me. "I'm sorry. I wish you'd told me sooner." Then he shrugged. "But how could you. I was never there, was I?" He leaned across to Ewen and ruffled his hair.

"My little Polly's been crying all night. Frightened to come to school because Granny Nothing's gone. I've never met the woman and I like her! I want her back!" This was Polly's mum, who looked just like an adult version of Polly.

Some of the other parents joined in the cry. "We want Granny Nothing!"

At the mention of her name Baby Thomas began to cry again.

"Oh, shut up, Thomas!" Dad moaned. "I'm going to get her back."

"Are you really, Dad?"

"If she can ever forgive me. . ." Dad said.

Chapter Eighteen

Next day the front page of the local paper carried the banner headline:

COME BACK GRANNY NOTHING

as well as the full-page story of the sit-down strike.

"Do you think that might bring her back?" Ewen asked me.

"I think it would have been better if we'd sat in the playground till she did come back!"

"But it started to rain," Ewen reminded me.

I tutted. "A little shower."

"It was a flaming thunderstorm!" Ewen pointed out the window just as a shaft of lightning lit up the sky. "And it's still going strong," he said. "Anyway, little Polly had her dancing lesson."

"And you had football." I was still disgusted at how quickly they had all dispersed. None of the teachers could move them. None of the parents could move them. But at the first bolt of lightning, they were up like a shot. "I don't think she'll come back. Why should she?"

Dad came into the room then, carrying Thomas. He was still sobbing, hadn't stopped crying since Granny Nothing had gone. Dad had made all his apologies to Ewen. If only Ewen had come to him, he had explained. Hadn't he known he would always come before any job? But Ewen hadn't. After all, hadn't Dad said often enough, "I can't lose this job. I simply can't."

"I want you to know now," he had told us today, over and over again, "that you come first. You and Stephanie, and Thomas. That's the only reason we've both been working so hard, for you three."

And Nanny Sue had gone too, for ever we hoped. She'd left a letter, too. Mum had read it out to us, barely keeping her giggles in check.

"I have given your children the best years of my life. . ." The best years of her life indeed! Nanny Sue was only nineteen! "And all the thanks I get is to be turfed out in favour of something vaguely resembling a woman. Very vaguely. Well, you shall all be very sorry. Because I am going to be rich and famous. Someone who heard my singing thought it was so good they secretly nominated me for a live audition on *Star-Maker*. And if you watch tonight you will see a new star being born. So there!!! And don't come to me for a ride in my limousine."

Mum couldn't stop giggling. "Nanny Sue on *Star-Maker*. But she's awful!"

"Yes," I agreed with glee. "We must remember to watch and have a good laugh at her."

Since teatime, Dad and Mum and Baby Thomas had been huddled in the kitchen talking. Now as he came into the room he had a broad smile on his face. "Is she back?" Ewen said, jumping from his chair.

"Who?" Dad asked.

"Granny Nothing."

Dad shook his head. "'Fraid not."

"Would you treat her better if she did come back?"

There was an accusation in my tone. Dad heard it and for a moment his smile disappeared.

"Why did you treat her so bad?" I asked him. "Was she bad to you when you were growing up?"

Dad patted the sobbing Thomas gently. It took him a moment to answer. "All my friends had nice, normal mothers. I had Godzilla. The teachers were frightened of her. The parents were frightened of her." Then his voice became very soft. "I just wanted her to be normal. I wanted her to be pretty. And she was always so loud. So cheeky. So ugly. I was ashamed of her."

"You were a snob, Dad," Ewen said.

"I was," Dad agreed at once. "I used to think I must have been adopted. Left on her doorstep when I was a baby. She was always so dirty, the house was so untidy. I was ashamed to bring any of my friends home. As soon as I was old enough, I left. Didn't write to her. Didn't contact her. Tried to pretend she didn't exist. I wanted to forget all about her. She found me though, and just asked me to let her know from time to time how my children were doing. So that was all I did. I feel so guilty now about that. But I was going to make sure that my children had everything I'd never had from her. A nice house, good clothes. I've worked hard for all those things for you. You know how hard I've always worked."

We knew, and now we knew why.

Dad went on wistfully. "But I'd forgotten how she could make me laugh, until I heard you laughing with her. I'd forgotten that all my pals had thought she was brilliant. And I'd forgotten too that I was never afraid when I was growing up because she was my mother, and she'd fight like a tigress to protect me. She was scared of nothing and nobody."

Yes, that was Granny Nothing all right.

"Would you be nicer to her if she came back?" I asked him again.

Dad smiled again. "More than that, I'd tell her how sorry I am. She's helped you, when I was too blind to see you needed help. And I'd tell her something else too." I waited in silence to hear what that "something else" was. "I'd tell her I loved her. That I'd always loved her."

Ewen groaned. "Oh, dead soppy."

"Anyway," I changed the subject abruptly before Dad started crying. "Why were you grinning when you came in here?"

Dad grinned again. "Why? Because Mum and I have come to a decision. I'm not going to look for another job."

"What? You mean you're going to be a . . . house husband?" Ewen tried to picture it, and couldn't.

Dad shook his head. "No, but I'm going into business for myself. If Dangerfield liked my project so much, why shouldn't I just keep it and use it myself? It'll be hard at first, but if things work out, Mum's going to give up her job and come in with me."

"You mean . . . you're not going back to Dangerfield Electronics?"

Dad laughed. "Nope! You know, this is what I've always wanted to do, I've just never had the courage before." He was beaming from ear to ear, looking exactly like Ewen when he'd scored a goal, or like Baby Thomas when he looked at Granny Nothing. I had never noticed how alike the men in my family were.

And who did I look like, I wondered? I pictured myself, in a frock with bad teeth, warts and corny, horny feet. Oh no, anything but that!

Mum came in from the kitchen then and she was smiling too. "I have a wonderful surprise for you," she said.

I jumped to my feet. "My granny's come back!"

Mum nodded.

"Yes," Mum said, holding the door open. "Your granny's back."

But it wasn't Granny Nothing who appeared. It was Granny Fielding.

Chapter Nineteen

I had never been so happy to see anyone in my life. I began to cry, couldn't stop myself. Granny Fielding threw her arms around me. Granny Fielding would know how to find Granny Nothing. Granny Fielding knew everything.

Ewen ran to her too. "Granny Fielding, you have to help us."

Granny Fielding smiled. She had the most beautiful teeth I had ever seen and her shiny hair had little droplets of rain sparkling through it. She was everything

Granny Nothing wasn't. She was clean. She smelled like summer roses. She dressed fashionably. Her voice was so soft. And as I hugged her close, breathing her in, a sudden horrible thought occurred to me.

Maybe Granny Fielding wouldn't want to share us with anyone. Maybe she would hate Granny Nothing too.

"So tell me about this Granny Nothing," she asked.

Did she really want to know? I looked at Ewen and knew he was thinking the same thing as me. Granny Fielding looked from one of us to the other. She was clever. She knew what we were both thinking. Suddenly, her nose crinkled and she smiled. "I think she sounds brilliant," she said. "Did she really scare those Rottweilers off? I could never have done that. I'm terrified of them too."

I screeched with delight. "You're not jealous."

She shook her head.

"Because, Granny, we don't love you any less."

"Well, of course, you don't," Granny Fielding said sensibly. "Love isn't like a cake, when you divide it up everyone gets a smaller share. No. Love's likes a sponge. It expands the more it absorbs. Anyway, children should have two grannies."

Now, everything was perfect. With Granny Fielding's help we would get Granny Nothing back.

Even Baby Thomas started to giggle. Happy for a moment.

And then, just as another flash lit up the sky, there was a sudden wail from next door's dogs.

"They're scared of the storm too," Granny Fielding said.

But I knew better. Only one person had ever made them wail like that. Granny Nothing.

"She's here," I said softly.

"Who's here?" Granny Fielding asked, holding us both at arm's length.

"Granny Nothing," Ewen said pointing into the garden. "Out there."

Granny Fielding didn't waste a minute. "Well, let's get her then."

We all pulled on raincoats and wellies. We even took Thomas who had wailed like the dogs when we tried to deposit him in his playpen.

We spread out in the pitch-black garden to look for her.

"Are you sure she's here?" Dad asked.

"I'm sure." But I wished I could see her. Why had she come back and not come in?

"She's gone," Dad said, and there was disappointment in his tone.

At that moment the lightning illuminated the whole garden, and there she was, pressed up against the garage, trying to hide from us.

Baby Thomas spotted her first and he yelled at the top of his voice, "Hell's Bells and Buckets!"

Chapter Twenty

We were back in the kitchen, drying off, and Granny Nothing had her enormous feet in a bucket of hot water. "Got to take care of your feet," she had said.

"But why were you hiding?" Ewen asked her.

Did she blush? I was sure she did. "I wasn't hiding," she insisted. "I was keeping out of the rain."

But she lied. "You were standing under the gutter," I reminded her. "You were getting soaked."

She didn't look up. "Och, I'll just steep my feet for a while and then I'll be on my way."

"You're not going!" Ewen cried. "Not after all we've done to get you back."

She was still looking at her feet but now she smiled. "Aye, that was nice. Made me feel good that, but. . ." she bent her head even lower so we couldn't see her face at all. "But that was before. . ." she swallowed. Was she swallowing a lump in her throat? Was Granny Nothing on the verge of crying? "Before. . ." Now, she looked up. She looked straight at Granny Fielding and there was genuine pleasure in her face. "Before your real granny came back. I saw you all through the window, hugging and laughing, and I thought, you don't need old Granny Nothing any more."

That was why she had hidden, I realized. She thought we wouldn't want her any more now Granny Fielding was here.

"But we do," Ewen said. "You have to stay."

She shook her head and sprayed everyone with rain. "Och, I've got too much to do to stay here. I'm a busy, busy woman."

"What have YOU got to do?" I asked her.

Granny Nothing looked affronted. "What do you mean? What have I got to do? I could be a superhero, for all you know. Is it a burd? Is it a plane? No, it's Granny Nothing away to avert another earthquake!"

I giggled. "You'd be more likely to cause one."

"Well, I'm going and that's all about it."

"But we need you." I knelt in front of her, and touched her hand. "I love Granny Fielding, but I can love you too."

Granny Fielding broke in now. "Of course you can.

And you must stay. Children should have two grannies. And I want to get back to Arizona." She smiled impishly. "I've met the most interesting man and I'd feel so much better if I knew you were looking after my darlings."

Granny Nothing shuffled her feet in the water. It almost caused a tidal wave. "Would you?" she murmured.

"And you have to stay now, this baby hasn't stopped crying since you left!"

And with that Mum deposited Baby Thomas into Granny Nothing's arms, where he'd been struggling to go ever since he'd first spotted her. He immediately gurgled and laughed and slapped his chubby hands all over Granny Nothing's face, and she loved it!

"You see," Mum said. "He adores you."

Granny Nothing didn't say a word at first. Holding Thomas close she let her eyes drift to Dad.

"Oh, you want to be coaxed?" Dad said.

"Dad!" Ewen and I reprimanded him at the same time.

"You want me to apologize? OK, I apologize. I'm sorry."

It didn't sound like any kind of apology to any of us and we all shouted at him. "DAD!"

He threw up his hands in defeat. "OK, OK. We need you. I'm going into business for myself. And we don't want any more nannies from hell. The children need you . . . their very own Granny Nanny. They love you. They trust you." He paused. "WE trust you. You have to stay."

It sounded more like an order to me. Dad looked at me and I mouthed to him, "You promised, Dad."

He looked at Granny Nothing for a long time. She

didn't look back. Then, taking everyone by surprise, he was suddenly on his knees beside her.

"Stay, Mother," he said. "In the last few days. I've learned more about my children than I've ever known since they were born. Thanks to you. I've learned more about you, too. Please, I want to learn more. Stay."

In a minute, I thought, they're going to hug. This is going to be a very precious moment. One to remember for ever.

I still didn't know Granny Nothing too well.

Instead of a hug, she gave Dad a push that sent him sprawling all over the floor. "Och, you big softie. Of course, I'm going to stay. I was only waiting for you to ask me nicely."

Mum suddenly checked her watch. "Goodness, we almost forgot to watch Nanny Sue on TV."

Dad switched on the set. "Just in time," he said.

Mum grinned. "Someone nominated her for *Star-Maker*, Granny Nothing, do you know anything about that?"

I glanced across at Granny Nothing. She had Thomas on her knee and a very innocent look on her face, at least she was trying to look innocent. "Me? Do I get the blame for everything in this house?"

Ewen and I tried not to giggle. Sure enough, we were just in time. There was Nanny Sue entering the audition, all girly and giggly the way she thought pop stars ought to be. She slipped a strap from her shoulder and pouted at the panel. "That's her trying to look sexy," Ewen whispered.

"About as sexy as a lizard with boils," I added.

"I didn't know Nanny Sue could sing," Granny Fielding said, all innocence.

We just couldn't stop the giggles then. Not me, not Ewen, and certainly not Granny Nothing. "And neither does she!" she roared with one of her belly laughs.

And that was when Nanny Sue did begin to sing. Or rather, she began to wail. It was meant to be a hit from the top ten. It sounded more like a cat being strangled very painfully. Nanny Sue danced about as she wailed. She couldn't dance either and she kept toppling over on her high heels. One of the judges sat open-mouthed in disbelief. Another had his hands over his ears. The third fell under the table laughing.

At last, one of them managed to get Nanny Sue to shut up. She grinned and waited for their praise.

"That was unbelievable," he said.

"Thank you," said Nanny Sue. The idiot.

"Who told you you could sing?" another asked her.

Her smile disappeared. "What are you trying to say?"

The third stopped laughing long enough to tell her, "You're rubbish."

Then he fell under the table again.

"I'm rubbish?"

"Ah, at least you agree with us."

"I'll have you know I was nominated for this show by someone who thought my voice was spectacular."

The judges all agreed with that. "It is. It's spectacularly awful."

"Whoever nominated you, dear, doesn't like you," one of them suggested. "In fact, I would say you have an enemy." Then he laughed so much he fell under the table too.

"Take my advice," the third judge said, managing at last to sit in his chair. "Go home, go back to your job. Hold on to that job, dear. Because you are to singing what Pavarotti is to Weightwatchers."

"Poor Nanny Sue," Mum said, feeling all sorry for her. "She is only nineteen. She's just a girl, you know."

No one else had the least bit of sympathy for her. Even Granny Fielding was laughing now.

Nanny Sue's face zoomed so close to the camera it filled the whole screen. Boy, she looked ugly this close up.

"Don't you worry. I know who's to blame for this. And I can assure you right now . . . I won't forget it! I'll be back."

I looked at Ewen. "She won't come back, will she?"

He looked at me. He didn't seem too sure about that. "And she's madder than ever."

"Och, don't worry about a thing," Granny Nothing said as we watched Nanny Sue being forcibly carried from the audition screaming her vengeance at us. "Granny Nothing's here to protect you now."

What a wonderful party we had that night. We danced and sang till midnight. Granny Nothing wobbled around the floor with Thomas clamped to her side.

I danced beside her for a while, and I asked her softly, because I had to know the answer, "The Shrunken Head in your case . . . is it real?"

She laughed so hard she shook all over. "It's real, all right. And there's a story behind it. And what a story it is. But that," she whispered, "is for another day."

Then she flashed her eyes and wobbled away from me.

As I watched her I thought how everything had changed since Granny Nothing had come into our lives. Changed for the better.

And I realized then that Granny Nothing was an angel.

A very fat angel, true, and one who would flatten any cloud she sat on, and frighten the life out of all the saints, but she was an angel nevertheless.

I was sleeping in Ewen's room while Granny Fielding was here, and Granny Nothing had moved in with Thomas. He wouldn't have it any other way. Wouldn't let her out of his sight.

"I don't think I've ever felt so happy in my whole life," I said as I snuggled under the covers.

"Yes, it's almost as good as the time the science teacher set fire to himself in class."

We both laughed and through the laughter we heard singing. Singing such as no one had ever heard before.

"I like wurums,
I like wurums,"

We could hear Baby Thomas gurgling.

"Here, son, you must be hungry."

And from the next room we could distinctly make out Baby Thomas chomping and chewing and then, he shouted his next new word.

"WURUMS!"

We looked at each other in horror.

"You don't think he's eating. . ." Ewen was almost sick at the thought of it.

"No," I said. "Of course not. He couldn't possibly be."

But with Granny Nothing, anything was possible.

Look out for the next book in this
flesh-wobblingly funny series!

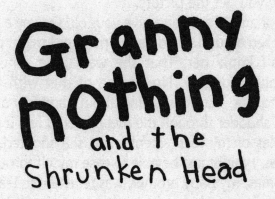

Granny
nothing
and the
Shrunken Head

"Help me, Steph. I'm stuck!"

Granny Nothing wiggled and wriggled and jammed
herself even further into the turnstile. "I'm definitely
stuck."

I froze. It was embarrassing enough to have to go
into town with your granny, any granny. But when that
granny happened to look like a rhinoceros in a frock, it
was a nightmare.

And the nightmare was getting worse. All we were
supposed to be doing was going into the toilets in the
railway station. But the toilets had a turnstile. You put in
your money and you slid through.

Or you were supposed to. Easy. Unless you are the size of Granny Nothing.

Imagine trying to thread an elephant through the eye of a needle.

Now you get the picture.

"Stephanie! Come and give your old Granny a shove."

I looked around. I had hoped perhaps I might pretend I didn't know her. That she was some other poor Stephanie's granny. No chance of that with Granny Nothing. She started wiggling about frantically and sent such a shudder through the metal I could feel it tickling the soles of my feet. "Stephanie!" she shouted. "Hold Thomas. I might just be able to ease myself through."

Thomas, my baby brother, was reluctant to leave her. He clung on to her hair. I just prayed he didn't start swearing. He had a habit of doing that. Copying Granny Nothing's language as well as her accent. He always sounded like a Scottish rugby player.

Thomas only started to scream. Screaming for his granny. She was delighted about that. "That boy loves his granny!" she said to anyone who would listen.

Already a crowd was forming at the entrance, gawping at her as if she was a fairground sideshow.

I am so embarrassed, I thought again. Why had I ever suggested going to the toilet? I should have known something like this would happen.

She began shaking, and sent shock waves through the turnstile, the walls and the whole station. It was like an earthquake.

The little attendant who had been hiding in his

glass-fronted office suddenly ran out and began to get excited. "Here! Here! Mrs, this is council property. You can't damage it."

Granny Nothing only shook herself again. "I've paid my twenty pence. I put it in the slot, and I haven't used the facilities. So shut your gob."

"Shut your gob!" Thomas agreed in a gruff Scottish accent.

"Thanks, son." She smiled over at him.

At that a woman shouted from the crowd. "I need to get in there too. Are you going to hurry up!" She was jumping from one foot to the other. I noticed then that a lot of the women were doing the same.

Granny Nothing just shrugged her shoulders. "It's not my fault I'm stuck."

It was at that moment Ewen emerged from the gents' toilets. He took one look at what was happening and did a U-turn back inside.

I was having none of that. "Ewen!" I yelled, pointing right at him. "Come and help your granny."

Granny Nothing saw him too. "Aye, come and help your old granny, son."

He had no choice, and together we pushed and we pulled but not one bit of difference did it make. She was still stuck.

"You're interfering with council business," the little attendant complained.

"I'll interfere with you in a minute if you don't shut up." Granny Nothing looked round the crowd who had built up. "Anybody got any bright ideas?"

"Dismemberment!" someone suggested helpfully. "We could get you out one bit at a time."

Granny Nothing shook and her whole body quivered. "Who said that! Just wait till I get out of here." She began scratching her head. "If only I'd listened when I was Houdini's assistant."

Ewen's jaw dropped. "You worked for Harry Houdini, the great escape artist?"

Granny Nothing guffawed with laughter. "Not at all. Archie Houdini. Master plumber. No relation."

There she goes again, I thought. More lies about the adventures she was supposed to have had. I never believed a word she said.

I felt like crying. Was she going to be stuck there for the rest of her life? Would we have to bring her food? Then another, more horrible thought raced into my mind. What was going to happen when she needed the toilet?

Aaargh! I was going to be sick.

"Ach, well," Granny Nothing said at last. "Nothing else for it." She poked the attendant. "Call the Fire Brigade."

"I am not calling out the Fire Brigade!" he said, stamping his feet. "The council wouldn't like that."

"Please yourself." Granny Nothing leaned back as if she was in the most comfortable place in the world. "I'm quite happy staying here. Got a lovely view." She called out to Ewen. "Away and get me a coffee and a doughnut."

There were yells from the dancing, impatient crowd,

desperate to get into the loo. They were already on their mobile phones. "Fire Brigade. And hurry!"

In the end the whole thing had to be dismantled. The attendant was nearly having a heart attack. "You're destroying council property," he kept yelling.

The firemen thought it was hilarious. So did Granny Nothing. Even when she was free, the turnstile was still wrapped round her like a steel hula-hula skirt.

"Suits me, doesn't it?" She wiggled and the whole thing made a very funny jangly noise.

So that was how we all ended up going to the hospital, in a fire engine, with Granny Nothing in a turnstile. The ladies' toilets were closed down – until further notice – and the attendant had to be sent home in shock.

The hospital was yet another embarrassment. No one could take their eyes off her.

"Have you never seen anybody in a toilet turnstile before!" she shouted at them all. I prayed to become invisible.

The doctor did a double take when he saw Granny Nothing standing there. (Well, she couldn't sit down, could she?) And then he laughed. He laughed so much the tears were streaming down his face. He kept wiping them away with the nurse's apron.

Granny Nothing watched him for a minute. She was getting annoyed at that laughter. A plan was hatching in that brain of hers. I could tell. All at once a very disgusting aroma began to fill the air.

Granny Nothing took a step back, away from the doctor. She pulled open the curtains of the cubicle. It was clear the smell had wafted into the waiting room. Everyone looked sick. Someone had passed out along the seats.

Granny Nothing ushered us outside. "Come along, children. The doctor couldn't help it. He must have ate something that disagreed with him last night."

The doctor's face went bright red. He looked at the nurse, already taking several steps away from him too. He looked at the patients. Their faces crinkled up in disgust. "That wasn't me!" he said loudly. He looked at Granny Nothing. "It wasn't me."

I knew it wasn't him, of course. We were used to Granny Nothing's strange smells. But I didn't say a thing. Everyone stepped away from the doctor until he was isolated.

Granny Nothing grinned. "That'll teach him to laugh at a poor old woman in a toilet turnstile," she said.

It took five firemen, two doctors and a welder to get her free of that turnstile.

"There ye go, another adventure with Granny Nothing," she said as we left the hospital.

And she was right there. Since Granny Nothing had come into our lives it had been one adventure after another.